A Book by Its Cover

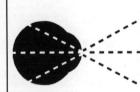

This Large Print Book carries the
Seal of Approval of N.A.V.H.

SECRETS OF MARY'S BOOKSHOP

A Book by Its Cover

Elizabeth Adams

THORNDIKE PRESS
A part of Gale, Cengage Learning

GALE
CENGAGE Learning·

Farmington Hills, Mich • San Francisco • New York • Waterville, Maine
Meriden, Conn • Mason, Ohio • Chicago

GALE
CENGAGE Learning·

LIBRARY OF CONGRESS CATALOGING-IN-PUBLICATION DATA

Adams, Elizabeth, active 21st century.
    A book by its cover / by Elizabeth Adams. — Large print edition.
        pages ; cm. — (Thorndike press large print Christian mystery) (Secrets of Mary's bookshop)
    ISBN 978-1-4104-6943-4 (hardcover) — ISBN 1-4104-6943-3 (hardcover)
    1. Booksellers and bookselling—Fiction. 2. Cape Cod (Mass.)—Fiction.
3. Large type books. I. Title.
PS3601.D3739B66 2014
813'.6—dc23   2014006581

Published in 2014 by arrangement with Guideposts, a Church Corporation

Printed in Mexico
1 2 3 4 5 6 7 18 17 16 15 14

Dear Reader,

When I was expecting my first child, my mom and I were speculating about what color eyes my daughter would have. Would she have brown eyes like me, or blue eyes like my husband? My mom started to list what eye colors various ancestors had, and mentioned that there were some unexpected combinations. . . . Then she confessed that, well, okay, there were some people in the family who said that her mother's eyes were an unlikely color — not because a fluke in genetics. There were rumors, she said, that her mother had a different father than her siblings.

I was shocked. *Was it really possible?* Had my grandmother really spent her entire life thinking one man was her father when they were not actually biologically related? How would that change her relationship with her parents? With her brothers and sisters?

That's where this story idea came from. What would happen, I wondered, if there was some evidence to suggest Mary and Betty had different fathers? How would that change how they felt about their mother? How would it change how they felt about each other? It was so fun to explore these ideas in *A Book by Its Cover.*

I don't have a sister, but I've always wished I did. I have two brothers, and I love them like crazy, but it's not the same as having a sister who could understand what I'm going through. It was really fun for me to explore the unique bond that Mary and Betty have and to live vicariously through them.

I love Cape Cod, and working on this book felt like coming home. Ivy Bay feels like a real place to me, and I hope it comes alive for you in these pages.

In Christ,
Elizabeth Adams

ONE

The autumn breeze clanged the Mary's Mystery Bookshop sign against its iron post. Branches bowed in the moonlight, their spindly shadows dancing along the vacant street. Mary Fisher drummed her fingers on a crumpled receipt as she watched a flurry of leaves blow past the window. Gus was curled up on the marble-topped front counter, purring in his sleep. Her rain boots were waiting for her by the front door.

With the tourist season over, few people walked the streets of Ivy Bay at night. Most of the fall visitors were gone by mid-November, and Ivy Bay ebbed back into a quiet village. Mary was grateful for a busy high season, but the late autumn was a welcome respite. A time for her to get caught up on her accounting . . . and her reading.

Last night, she'd started a new mystery called *The Cellar Door* and she'd already devoured sixteen chapters. Now the novel rested under her desk lamp, open, beckoning her to read just one more page before she finished totaling last month's invoices.

She should just get through the receipts, and then she could finish the book with no interruptions. She reached for the next invoice on her stack, but her eyes traveled back to the book. Just one more page wouldn't hurt.

Lady Chantal Vincent was creeping down the staircase of the old manor, into a basement that hadn't been used in more than thirty years. The door groaned when Lady Vincent opened it, and Mary wanted to shout at the woman: "Run! Hide! Do anything except walk through the arched doorway!" Inspector Deniau was hiding in the cellar, and he wouldn't play nice. Lady Vincent knew too much.

Mary looked up when she got to the end of the chapter. She shook her head, closed the book, and set it aside. The cat stirred and stretehed the counter. "Rough day, huh, Gus?" He settled his head on his paws and closed his eyes, ignoring her.

The computer screen glowed on the high countertop. Her screen saver flashed pictures in and out as a slide show. A photo of Mary and her sister Betty at the church picnic on Little Neck Beach faded away to a grainy shot of a young Mary, Betty, their mother, and their mother's best friend, Tabitha Krause, standing on the steps of Mary's grandmother's home. It was the house where their mother had grown up, and where Mary and her sister had stayed during their childhood visits to Ivy Bay. Mary smiled for a moment at the memory of her mom, who had returned to Ivy Bay for one last visit a year before she passed away. Mary had come to Cape Cod to see her during that trip, and they had spent much of their time reminiscing about the old days with Tabitha. Being back in Ivy Bay had brought great joy to Esther Nelson. She'd recounted such happy stories about growing up in town; and in telling the stories, she seemed younger.

The picture faded away, and Mary nudged the mouse to reawaken her accounting software. As she stared at the numbers, they seemed to swim together on the screen. She eyed the rust-colored spine of her novel, and she fought the urge to find out what happened next.

The receipt in her hand was for three used books she'd purchased last week from Jayne Tucker at Gems and Antiques. She quickly typed in the numbers and set the receipt onto the small stack of completed invoices. The stack she'd yet to input seemed to tower in comparison.

If only Lady Vincent could find out where the inspector had locked away her husband. He was still alive, Mary knew it. Perhaps Lord Vincent was hidden in the cellar.

Goose bumps pricked on Mary's arms. She had to find out what happened next. Just one more chapter, and then she would finish the invoices. She reached for the book.

Her cell phone trilled, and Mary dropped the book onto the counter and glanced toward the dark store window as if someone would be there watching her. No one was there, of course, but she was suddenly on edge. She shouldn't be reading these mysteries at night when she was alone.

Betty's name flashed onto the screen. "Hey, Bets," she said as she put the phone to her ear.

"I was just checking on you." Her sister sounded worried. "It's supposed to storm tonight."

Mary glanced toward the wall clock, but with all the lights in the bookshop already turned off except for her small desk lamp, she couldn't see it. She'd only planned to work for an hour after closing and then go straight home for dinner, but Lady Vincent's plight had made her lose track of time.

"What time is it?" she asked.

"It's almost nine."

"I'm so sorry." Mary sighed. "I got distracted."

"Do you have to finish what you're doing tonight, or can it wait till tomorrow?"

Mary's gaze swept over the receipts on the counter to the stack of books on the floor beside her, waiting to be inventoried. The children's area was a wreck after a group of first graders had raided the store on a field trip this afternoon. Books were everywhere, chocolate was smeared across the wall, the rug had been partially torn out of the bathtub that acted as a cozy reading place, and there were unidentified sticky patches on the floor. She didn't have the energy to put away all the books or clean up tonight. Tomorrow morning, she would ask her employee Rebecca to help her.

She ran her fingers down the spine of *The Cellar Door.* "I just want to finish these receipts. I can finish the rest tomorrow."

"I made tuna casserole for dinner, if you're still hungry." Mary heard the refrigerator door close on Betty's end of the line. "And I saved a bit of the leftover tuna for Gus."

"I see how it is." Mary nudged the cat

11

with her elbow. He looked up, yawned, and went back to sleep. "You weren't really calling to ask me to come home. You just miss Gus."

Betty laughed. "That'll be the day." Betty hadn't been thrilled with the idea of Mary bringing a cat into her home at first, and she sometimes still pretended to be put out by his presence, but Mary knew her sister had grown to love the little rascal.

Mary eyed the receipts again. If she focused, she could get them all done before ten. "I should be home within the hour."

"Okay, but I might be tempted to eat the rest of the casserole by myself."

Mary laughed again. "Make that a half hour."

There was a brief pause on the phone, and for a second she thought Betty had hung up. When her sister spoke again, her voice was tinged with concern. "Seriously, Mar. If you're not home in an hour, I might just have to come and get you in my robe and slippers."

Mary smiled at the thought of her sophisticated sister plodding down to the bookshop in her robe. "The door is locked, and I've got Gus here to protect me. I'll be home before ten," she said, and ended the call.

Ever since the break-in at her store when she first moved back to Ivy Bay, Betty occasionally got nervous when Mary was alone at the shop at night, but Mary had quickly forgiven Kip for what he'd done. He hadn't meant any harm, and now they were friendly. Still, even though she was safe in the store, it felt good to have someone worry about her. Betty helped anchor Mary, especially during those times when her heart ached for John. With her husband gone, she thanked the Lord every day for His love and for the gift of her sister.

She picked up another receipt to input the information into the computer, but she couldn't resist the pull of the story. It was no use. She wouldn't get any more work done until she found out what happened to Lady Vincent. After she finished it, she wouldn't start another novel until she was caught up with her accounting. That would be good motivation to complete it. For now, she'd head home.

With a few clicks of her mouse, Mary shut down her computer, and she stuffed the book into her handbag. If she was going to read, she'd rather do it at home in her bed, after a full plate of casserole.

In the dim light of her desk lamp and the streetlamp that shone through the front window, she pulled the hem of her khaki pants over her boots. Then she went to the back room and grabbed her blue fleece-lined rain jacket and buttoned it as she walked back toward the front of the store. She grabbed her purse and Gus's cat carrier, clicked off the desk lamp, then scooped Gus off the countertop. The cat replied with a grumpy meow.

She scratched him behind his ears. "Don't you start lecturing me."

Mary started to put Gus into his carrier, but she heard something shuffle outside. She stepped back, looking out the window, and in the silvery light of the streetlamp, she could see a shadow on the other side of the door. Strange that someone would be coming to her door so late at night.

Her fingers ran down the soft gray fur on Gus's back. As she stepped toward the door again, she clutched Gus a little closer to her chest, though she knew it was crazy. There was no reason for her to be paranoid. Surely she wasn't the only one in Ivy Bay working late tonight.

But then the person outside jiggled her doorknob.

Mary took a step back, staring at the knob. Perhaps this person was luring her to the door, like the inspector had done to Lady

Vincent in her novel. Perhaps whoever it was had seen her light on and knew she was still here.

Gus snuggled up closer to her chest, purring.

"You're supposed to guard me, buddy," she whispered, rubbing under his neck. Part of her wanted to open the door, but she hesitated. Who would be trying to get into her store now? If Rebecca or Henry decided to come by, they would call first so they wouldn't startle her. The naked branches of the tree outside the shop cast eerie shadows on the wall behind the counter.

She heard a thud outside the door. Perhaps she should call Betty back. With Gus cradled in her left arm, she retrieved her cell phone from her pocket, but just as she began to dial, she realized she didn't hear anything more. She waited for several seconds, straining to detect any movement outside the door, but all she heard was the sign clanging against its post.

"Do you think they left?" she asked Gus. He nudged his nose against her arm.

"I think so too."

With her phone in one hand and Gus cradled in the other, Mary glanced back out the window. The branches still danced in the wind, but the person was gone.

She stepped toward the door, and for a moment, she wondered if, like Lady Vincent, she was about to walk into a terrible trap. But then a Scripture verse flashed through her mind. *For God did not give us a spirit of timidity,* the verse said, *but a spirit of power, of love and of self-discipline.* It was from 2 Timothy, and it reminded her that not only was she being silly, but she also wasn't relying on God.

God wanted her to be smart, but He also didn't want her to be afraid. He was in control. She took a deep breath, reached for the door handle, and turned it.

Two

There was no Inspector Deniau outside Mary's Mystery Bookshop, of course. No one was there. Instead, there was a small cardboard box on the other side of the door. Mary laughed into the darkness. The story in *The Cellar Door* was playing with her mind, making her paranoid. Whoever had been here was just dropping off a box of books.

Many people wanted to sell their used books, but sometimes, someone would donate them to Mary. No one had ever dropped off books after the store closed, but if the books were decent in both condition and content, she wouldn't argue with a donation, no matter how late it was delivered. Going through old books was one of the many things she loved about this job. Old books had a peculiar, familiar smell, and she loved the thick paper and sturdy binding you didn't seem to get in new books these days. Plus, old books could sometimes be true gems, on topics you would never find in a publisher's catalog today. She had found some truly delightful British gardening mysteries that were long out of print at an estate sale last month.

Gus jumped out of Mary's arms and scrambled back into the warmth of the store. It was late, but she couldn't go home quite yet. Not until she saw what the person had left her.

The cardboard box was about a foot tall and maybe two feet wide. She bent to lift it, hoping it wasn't too heavy, but she picked it up easily and carried it inside. She flipped the lights back on with her elbow and set the box gently on the front counter.

There was no address on the outside of the box, or any other information that would identify the donor, so she took a pair of scissors from a cubbyhole behind the counter and cut off the clear packing tape. Inside, bright pieces of pink-and-mint-green-striped paper were wrapped around eight hardback books. There was no card or note among them to say who had delivered the books.

She lifted the first book out of the box and ran her fingers over the beautifully illustrated dust jacket. It appeared to be a children's book, and the jacket showed a boy building a sand castle on a beach. It was done in watercolors, with light, delicate strokes. The image was amazingly detailed, with layers of color creating an almost luminous cast to the sand, and many rich shades of blue — from deep turquoise to bright cerulean to the lightest robin's egg — mingled to make the sea almost sparkle. Mary could see that it must have taken quite a long time and a great deal of skill to create such an image.

She opened the cover and flipped through the pages. The book was indeed a children's story called *The Sand Castle* and was written by a Matthew Parker. The publication date was 1956. She turned the pages gently. They were in wonderful condition, not soiled or stained in any way, and the book smelled mercifully free of must. It would be wonderful to add more vintage children's books to her shelves. She would read it carefully tomorrow to make sure the story was good, and then she would add it to the children's nook.

Mary put the book aside and lifted out the next book in the stack. This was a novel, from the same decade, called *The View from the Lighthouse.* The author was listed as Dara Knoll. It was a mystery, and the cover showed a long stretch of rocky beach with a lighthouse perched at the top of a craggy cliff. It was a very different sort of book, but the cover was painted in the same watercolor style. The colors in the image blended as perfectly and as beautifully as they had on the children's book cover.

Gus hopped up on the counter and poked his nose into the box. He sniffed, then started to climb into the box, and Mary gently brushed him aside and reached for the next book. He let out a whine and then began to lick his paw, as if to show Mary he didn't care to see what was in the box, anyway.

The next book in the stack was a novel too, with the title *Sea Breeze* in a bold navy-blue font. The jacket showed a young couple holding hands as they strolled along the beach. Behind them was an opulent stone mansion with tall sea grasses as its lawn. Mary stared at the mansion for a long time. The style of the art was the same as the previous covers; in fact, as she scanned the rest of the books in the box, they all seemed to be done by the same artist. But that wasn't the only thing that caught her eye. The cover looked familiar to her. She had seen this book somewhere before. In fact — she looked back at the other books

— they all looked vaguely familiar. But she knew she had seen this one. She just wished she knew where.

The ring of her cell phone startled her once again. She pulled it back out of her pocket and saw Betty's name on the screen again. "I'm on my way," she insisted, still studying the beautiful painting on the book cover.

"I'm headed out in my bathrobe now," Betty said. She was teasing, but the pinched tone in her voice told Mary that she had been worried.

"There's no need to scandalize the neighbors," Mary said, and Betty laughed. She put *Sea Breeze* back into the box and stood up. "I'm sorry, Bets. I got distracted by a late-night delivery."

"More books?"

"No." Mary laughed. "It was a rope and a funny looking candlestick."

This time, Betty laughed with her. "It's a good thing I love you."

"I'm very glad of it."

Mary looked down at the box one more time before she turned off the light. She was certain she'd seen the cover of *Sea Breeze* a long time ago, but she couldn't recall where it had been.

■ ■ ■ ■

"You probably did see the books before," Betty said as she spread strawberry jam on her toast the next morning at breakfast. "Maybe at a bookstore in Boston, or when you worked at the library." Betty's honey-blonde hair was pulled back in a barrette, and she wore an olive cashmere sweater and perfectly pressed khaki pants. She was also wearing the diamond earrings that her husband, Edward, had given her as a wedding present. It wasn't like Betty to wear something so flashy, and with a pang, Mary realized today would have been Edward's sixty-ninth birthday. Mary made a mental note to do something special for Betty today. "You've certainly seen plenty of books in your life," Betty added.

Mary sipped her milky coffee. Betty was right, of course. Mary could have encountered those books thousands of different ways. "It's going to drive me crazy until I figure it out, though," Mary said. The cranberry bog behind their home glowed a brilliant red, filled with ripe berries just waiting to be harvested. Very soon, the bogs around here would all be flooded, and then they would be winter brown again.

"Were the books at all valuable?" Betty said, taking a dainty bite of her toast. The *Ivy Bay Bugle* lay open next to her plate, and Mary could see her sister was reading about a pie company in Centerville that had so much business it had already stopped taking orders for Thanksgiving.

"I don't think so." Mary set her coffee cup down. Truthfully, she hadn't really looked into it, but she hadn't seen anything unusual about the books except the fact that she recognized the covers. She'd had a little trouble falling asleep last night, trying to figure out where she'd seen them. She'd been so distracted she hadn't even finished reading *The Cellar Door.*

She'd seen thousands of book covers over her career, but these stood out.

Mary and Betty fell into a comfortable silence, and as Betty turned back to her newspaper, Mary leaned back in her chair. She could see the cover from *Sea Breeze* in her mind's eye. She could see it sitting there on a bookshelf. She remembered the way the cliffs faded off into the distance under the type on the spine of the book. She'd seen it, stared at it even, fascinated by how the gradations of color eventually, almost imperceptibly, gave way to white. Yes, she had definitely seen that spine on a bookshelf, but she couldn't remember which shelf. The memory was lodged back in her brain, somewhere between the place where she'd left her house key last week and the title of the play her granddaughter Daisy was in at school. Now she'd have to wait until the information about the books sifted itself out.

Betty ate her last bite of toast and closed the newspaper, then took her plate to the sink to rinse. The morning sun washed over the white tile countertops and made Betty's collection of cobalt-blue jars glow.

Mary watched her sister place her plate in the dishwasher and wipe her hands on the hand-embroidered dishtowel. Betty had bought the towel at a yard sale over the summer, and Mary had been surprised that Betty would be interested in an old used towel, until she saw how perfectly it complemented the colors in the kitchen. Betty had quite an eye for detail. "Would you have time to look at the books today, Bets?" Mary asked. "Maybe you would recognize the covers."

"I have a meeting at church this morning to coordinate the Thanksgiving food drive, but I can stop by the store after that."

"Sounds great." Mary twisted the coffee cup in her hands. Had one of her schoolteachers had those books in her classroom when Mary was a child? She shook her head. It would come to her. She stood up and had started to move toward the sink when her cell phone rang. Mary put her cup down on the counter and dug her phone out of her purse.

"Who is it?" Betty asked, as she added soap to the dishwasher.

Mary glanced down at the Boston area code. She didn't recognize it. "I don't know." She sat back down at the table and answered it.

"Hello, is this Mary Fisher?" the caller said in a thick Boston accent.

"Yes." She tried to place the voice. She'd lived in Boston for many years and still had many friends there, but this man didn't sound familiar.

"This is Harrison Greer from *Cape Cod Living,*" the caller said. At least Mary thought he said Harrison. The man spoke so fast it was hard to say for certain.

Betty sat back down at the table, studying her. Mary glanced over at Betty, raising her eyebrows. Why was the lifestyle magazine calling *her?*

"What?" Betty mouthed.

She put her hand over the speaker. "It's *Cape Cod Living.*"

Betty's eyes grew wide at the name of one of her favorite magazines.

"Well, Ms. Fisher, I was driving through Ivy Bay last week researching a story, and I stumbled onto your bookshop. I grabbed a business card because it's completely charming, and our readers —"

He paused and started talking to someone else. The phone crackled. "I'm sorry. Ms. Fisher?"

"I'm still here. Please, call me Mary."

"We just had an opening for our January edition, which is due" — Harrison clicked his tongue for several seconds — "next Monday."

"What sort of opening?"

"I guess that's important information too," he said with a quick laugh. "I'm moving a little too fast this morning."

There was more talking in the background before he replied. "Every month, we feature a small business on the Cape. Something quaint and charming. A place that the locals love. We want Mary's Mystery Bookshop to be our January pick."

She swallowed hard. "You want to feature my shop?"

She glanced over at her sister, and Betty teetered slightly on her chair. Her eyes were wide, her lips puckered. It almost looked like she might faint.

"If you don't object," Harrison said.

"Of course not," she reassured him. "It's just so . . . unexpected. I'm thrilled."

"I'll need to bring a photographer back out with me, ASAP. And I'll need to interview you too." He rustled some papers. "What does tomorrow look like for you?"

"Tomorrow?"

She glanced at Betty, and her sister nodded her head with a mixture of enthusiasm and panic. She would definitely need Betty's help to get the bookshop ready for a photographer.

"Around nine, maybe?" he asked.

Mary took a deep breath. "Tomorrow at nine would be great."

She hung up and looked at Betty, wide-eyed.

"Let's head to the store now. I can be a bit late to my meeting."

Mary nodded wordlessly. They had a lot of work to do before nine tomorrow.

THREE

Mary released Gus from his carrying case, and he scurried off to the back room where his food was. Minutes later, Betty hurried into the shop and stood in front of the white marble counter, a stack of *Cape Cod Living* issues in her arms. Mary sat down on the stool behind the counter and moved aside the receipts she'd been working on last night so her sister could set the magazines on the countertop.

"Research?" Mary asked with a smile as she picked up one of the issues and thumbed through it.

"You know I always have these around," Betty said, grinning.

Mary's arm bumped the box of books at the other end of the counter. She started to move the box to the floor, but then stopped. "Actually, before we get too involved, could you take a quick look at these books?"

"I will," Betty said, digging through the

stack of magazines. "I promise. But first things first." She flipped open the cover of the September issue and ran her manicured fingernails down the headshots and short biographies of each editor and writer. She stopped when her fingers crossed Harrison Greer's name.

"This is your man."

Mary looked at Harrison's shaved head and cocky smile. He was probably in his midthirties, a few years younger than her son Jack. "He looks friendly enough."

Betty flipped the pages until she found the featured business in September and tapped it. "Look at what a nice job they did on this inn."

The spread showed three gorgeous pictures of an elegant bed-and-breakfast in Nantucket. It was a sunny yellow, and a cobblestone lane led to the ivy-green door. The inn overlooked a stretch of golden-white beach, and the garden behind the house was a riot of colors, blooming with heirloom roses, hydrangeas, clematis, morning glories, and sunflowers. In another picture, the country breakfast table was set with fine china, a sterling silver coffee set, and cloth napkins wrapped with silver rings. Bowls of fruit and candles decorated the table's center, and beyond the table, open

French doors gave guests a sweeping view of the dunes along Nantucket Sound.

Mary smoothed her fingers over the page. "It's lovely."

"And look at this tea shop in Wellfleet," Betty said as she opened another issue.

The colorful photograph in the center showed a quaint shop decorated with lace curtains, a display of delicate teacups, and an enormous floral arrangement sitting on top of a weathered hutch. A light mint-colored paint accented the white wainscoting along the walls.

Mary pointed at the hutch. "The flowers are a nice touch."

Betty looked toward the reading area at the back of Mary's store, by the fieldstone hearth. Two comfortable armchairs, upholstered in ivory twill, sat in front of the fireplace, and the throw on each chair was knitted in the colors of the Atlantic.

"We can get flowers and put them on the table between the chairs," Betty suggested.

Mary nodded, catching her enthusiasm. "And perhaps a small bouquet on the countertop."

Betty stepped toward the opening to the children's area. "We can put another arrangement by the children's books —" Her mouth dropped open at the sight in front of her. "What happened in here?"

"A school field trip," Mary replied simply. There was no need for further explanation.

Betty stepped back toward the counter, flipping rapidly through the pages again. "I'll have to update the window display." Betty gestured at the front window of the store, which was decorated with an autumnal theme. Betty had gathered golden, red, and orange leaves from nearby trees and arranged them artfully around a series of fall-themed books. "I'll try to come up with something that would look right in January. Oh, and we should spruce up the patio —"

"I don't think we need to do all that."

Betty didn't even hear her. "And we'll have to clean the walls and the floors, and maybe even touch up the paint."

Mary started to argue, but then stopped herself. She knew better than to get in Betty's way when she had a vision for how things should look. And she was grateful for the help. Still, she gazed at the box of books she'd left on the counter last night. She'd hoped to spend some time trying to find out more about them today.

"We should clean up the children's area before we do anything else."

"We don't have to make it perfect, Bets."

"I suppose not." She gave a light sigh, and

then her face brightened again. "But we can make it close to perfect."

"Deal."

Betty sniffed. "What is that smell? It's wonderful."

Mary sniffed too, and detected the scent of sweet cinnamon rolls. Sweet Susan's Bakery was next door to the shop; Susan must have just taken a fresh batch out of the oven.

"Susan must be getting ready to open for the day." Mary glanced at her watch. It was nine. "Which means Rebecca will be here to help us in an hour."

"I'm going to have to stop by the bakery later and get one of those rolls," Betty said. "How do you smell that all day? I'd be so tempted."

"I have my days," Mary said ruefully. The truth was, she was tempted by the delicious aromas coming from the bakery most days, but she tried to limit her treats.

"Oh, Mary, just think of the publicity." Betty closed the magazine and gave a clap with her hands. "People will come from all over the East Coast to visit your store."

Mary smiled at her sister's enthusiasm. It was exactly what she needed.

Mary saw Dorothy Johnson walk by the window of the shop, headed toward the church. Dorothy was involved with a lot of committees and groups at Grace Church, and Mary would bet she was headed to Betty's meeting.

"What time is your meeting at the church, Bets?"

"There are advantages to being the chair-woman." Betty walked back to the book-shelves and started to straighten a row of books. "They can't start without me." She looked around the shop again. "Still, I should get going. I'll be back after the meet-ing, and I'll bring some things to help spruce up the shop."

Mary gave her a wave, and the bell over the door chimed as Betty stepped out into the clear fall day. "I'll be here."

After Betty left, Mary arranged the maga-zines into a neat stack on the counter and then flipped the sign hanging in the front door to announce that they were open. Re-becca had called to say she would be a few minutes late, but Mary didn't mind. Re-becca had a seven-year-old daughter, and Mary remembered what it was like getting a child off to school in the mornings. She decided to start cleaning on her own. She edged through the picket gate to the chil-dren's nook, and she couldn't help but

laugh. Yesterday's little gaggle of first graders had been adorable, but they had left a
path of destruction behind them on the pine
floorboards and coral-colored walls and
white pedestal bathtub Betty had bought
for the store as a unique reading space.
Fortunately, none of the children's damage
was permanent. She could wipe off the
chocolate and clean up the candy wrappers
and books. Between her, Rebecca, and
Betty, they could have this area cleaned up
soon, and then they could tackle the rest of
the shop.

She began picking books out of the tub to
reshelve and got much of the children's area
put back into shape, but she looked up
when the door chimed. Her first customer
of the day was a pretty woman in her early
twenties, a striped scarf wrapped around
her dark turtleneck. Her black hair was
pulled back in a slick ponytail, and her dark
jeans flared over black boots. She carried a
portfolio in her arms.

"Good morning." Mary tucked her short
hair back over her ears as she greeted the
woman. "How can I help you?"

"My name is Karly Sundin." She shifted
the portfolio to her other arm to shake
Mary's hand. She had a firm handshake and
a wide smile. "I'm looking for a job."

"I'm Mary Fisher." Mary searched Karly's dark green eyes, but she didn't recognize her. "Are you from around here?"

Karly shook her head, but her smile didn't falter. "No, though I wish I were." She held up her portfolio. "I'm staying here for a few months, taking pictures on the Cape." Words tumbled out of her mouth so quickly Mary had to listen carefully to keep up, but Karly didn't seem nervous. She radiated a kind of warm confidence that made Mary like her instantly.

"How lovely. Are you a professional photographer?" Mary asked.

"One day . . ." Karly sighed. "At the moment, I can only manage one day a week, so I spend all day Sunday shooting. But right now, I'm actually looking for part-time work. I was hoping to find something at one of these adorable shops on Main Street. Are you hiring? I love books."

Mary shook her head regretfully. "It's the slow season for most of the businesses on Cape Cod. Unfortunately, that includes our store. But —"

Karly nodded. "I understand." She pulled her portfolio closer to her chest and turned to leave. "Thanks, anyway. I appreciate your time."

"Wait, Karly." Mary reached out, touch-

35

ing Karly's elbow. "Jayne Tucker at Gems and Antiques mentioned the other day that she was looking for some part-time help for the next month or so." Jayne and Rich were busy getting things ready to shut down; they would spend up to a month in the winter in Europe, hunting for finds to stock their store.

"Oh, that's wonderful." The smile returned. "Thank you." Karly motioned to the bookshelf beside her. "This bookshop is really beautiful." She glanced around the room until her gaze rested on the lavishly illustrated books about Cape Cod. "I read a lot. About history and art and photography, of course, but other things too. I always thought walking into a bookstore was like escaping into another world."

"Yes, it is a bit like that," Mary agreed. She hoped her store was a place of refuge and exploration for her customers. She wished she had an opening, but she was already stretching her budget to keep Rebecca employed through the late autumn and winter. They chatted for several minutes about their favorite books, and the more they talked, the more Mary liked the young woman's passion, as well as her determination. Karly hoped to move to a big city and show her work in galleries someday, but recognized she'd probably have to work a full-time job to pay the bills.

"I've taken several shots around Ivy Bay that I think I might show to a gallery owner I know in Brooklyn," Karly said. "To see if they might work for his space."

"Really?" Mary pointed at the portfolio in Karly's hands. "I'd love to see those."

"Sure." Karly followed Mary to the counter, and Mary moved the stack of magazines to the floor and pushed the box of old books to the side. Karly unzipped the portfolio, and Mary began looking through Karly's beautiful photographs. There was a picture of an old lighthouse and one of a coastal inlet at sunset, but the ones Mary found most intriguing were the shots around Ivy Bay and in other small towns on the Cape — the narrow alleys that threaded through the fishermen's shanties down by the Ivy Bay marina, the sparse beauty of the windswept beach under a steel-gray November sky, the candid shots of the people strolling down cobbled streets under glorious autumn foliage.

Mary smiled when she looked back up at Karly. "These are marvelous."

A faint red crept up Karly's cheeks. "Thank you."

Mary turned the page and saw a striking

photograph of an old man, his craggy face turning toward the sun, which was just starting to peek over the horizon in the distance. He was sitting on what looked to be a wooden porch, and the early morning light bathed his face in a glow that emphasized each line on his face.

"This is stunning."

"Thanks." She gave a sly smile.

"They're all really good," Mary said. "Actually, your coastal pictures remind me a bit of some paintings I saw just last night." She opened the box and pulled out the top two books. "Aren't these lovely?" She pulled the dust jackets off the books and spread them out carefully on the marble counter.

Karly reached for the closer dust jacket, the cover for *Sea Breeze*. Her green eyes widened. She looked back up at Mary. "Where did you get these?"

Mary started. That was a strange reaction. Why did Karly seem so surprised to see these covers?

"Someone left them outside my door last night." Mary pulled out one of the books, examining the lighthouse on the cover again. She glanced back up at Karly. "Are you familiar with them?"

"I-I," she stuttered, then took a breath and

continued. "I think I might have seen them before."

Mary watched her, trying to gauge her reaction. "I think I've seen them before as well," she said slowly. "But I can't for the life of me remember where."

Karly pushed the book jacket back toward Mary. Lines crinkled Karly's forehead.

"Are you feeling okay?" Mary asked.

Karly visibly forced a smile, and then she seemed to recover. "I'm great," she said, cheerful as before. "Those covers are really beautiful. I wish I had talent like that. Thank you for showing them to me."

Mary wondered at the change in the young woman after she'd seen the books. Or had Mary said something that startled the young woman? She quickly reviewed her last words but couldn't think of anything she said that might offend Karly. No, Karly knew something about the books that she wasn't telling Mary. Could she have dropped them off last night? But she'd asked where Mary had gotten them and had seemed genuinely surprised to see them. Would she have reacted that way if she'd been the person who'd delivered them?

Karly turned toward the door. "Well, I should probably go. Gotta keep pounding the pavement." She laughed a little, but to

Mary, it sounded forced. She didn't meet Mary's eye.

Karly opened the front door, and a cool breeze, along with the smell of cinnamon rolls, stole through the bookstore. "I'll go talk to your friend at the antique store. Thanks again, Mrs. Fisher."

Mary wanted to stop her from leaving, ask what was wrong, but she didn't want to force the subject. "Please tell Jayne I sent you."

Karly thanked Mary one last time and then hurried out the door. Mary watched Karly rush across the street, toward Gems and Antiques. Then she carefully put the covers back on the books and laid them gently in the box. What a strange reaction to an old collection of books. Who brought these old books to her last night, and what did Karly Sundin know about them?

Mary turned and surveyed the shop around her. She didn't have time today to track down the answers to either of these questions. She needed to mop the floor and dust all the shelves, tabletops, and light fixtures before tomorrow morning. Then there was the glass display under the front counter to clean and windows to wash. She should straighten the back room too, just in case the editor went there. For the first time in a long while, she hoped it would be a slow day for the shop.

As she started toward the back room to retrieve the duster, the door opened again. This time, her employee Rebecca Mason walked into the shop. "I'm so sorry I'm late." Rebecca stopped for a deep breath before she took off her long overcoat. "Ashley forgot her lunch so I had to run back home to get it." She walked toward the back room and hung up her coat.

"It's no problem at all," Mary said, nodding back toward the children's area. "We had a field trip in here after you left yesterday, so we'll have plenty to do this morning."

Rebecca stepped around the display case and set her purse in one of the cubbyholes under the white counter. Then she sat on her swivel chair.

Rebecca eyed the open box of books sitting on top of the counter. "Where did those come from?"

Mary shrugged. "Someone left them on our doorstep last night."

"Hmm . . ." Rebecca leaned over and twisted the box around like she was looking for a return label. "That's a bit odd, don't you think?"

Mary nodded. "I thought so too, especially

since they are such beautiful old books. All of them were published in the 1950s."

Rebecca scooted her chair up to the desk. "If you want, I can inventory them."

Mary leaned against the counter, pointing at a pile of books stacked up beside Rebecca's chair. "Actually I was hoping you could inventory all those books this morning so we can shelve them as soon as possible."

"Sure," Rebecca said, though Mary could see the questioning in her eyes.

"You see," Mary began — she couldn't help the smile creeping up on her lips — "*Cape Cod Living* is coming to do a feature story on us tomorrow morning."

Rebecca let out a whoop and then sprang from her seat, rushing around the counter to hug Mary. "So they did call you."

"What do you mean? Did you know about this?"

Rebecca smiled guiltily. "Someone called from *Cape Cod Living* yesterday, and you were out at lunch, but I knew you'd be excited so I gave him your cell number."

"And you didn't tell me?"

"I decided it wasn't my place." She swiveled a little in her chair. "Besides, I thought it would be more fun for you to get the news from them."

Mary put her hands on her hips and shook

her head, but she wasn't really frustrated. She was too excited to be upset. "Well, they're coming here. Tomorrow."

"That's fantastic!"

Betty rushed back into the store, carrying a bag from Meeting House Grocers. She set it down on the counter and started unpacking rags and cleaning supplies. "There's no time to dillydally, ladies."

"That was a quick meeting," Mary said, laughing.

"How much is there to say? We put bins in the church foyer every Thanksgiving. It's not rocket science." Betty handed Mary a bottle of cleaner and a package of rags. "Let's divide and conquer."

Rebecca moved back to her seat. "I'll see if I can get these books inventoried before lunch."

"I can work on dusting," Betty volunteered.

"Hey, Bets, first, can you come take a look at these books I was telling you about?" Mary motioned Betty toward the cardboard box on the counter, pulling it toward her. "I wanted to see if you recognized any of them."

Betty joined her at the counter, and Mary pushed back the pink-and-mint-colored paper and picked up a stack of the hardback books, piling them up on the front counter. The top book was one of the children's books. It had a boy and girl playing in the waves on the beach.

As Mary looked down at waves, and then down the colorful spines on the counter, and then back at her sister, an image began to form in her mind. Her heart began to race as she glanced once more at Betty and then back at the books.

Betty cocked her head. "Is something wrong?"

"I'm starting to remember." She quickly pulled all the books from the box and began standing them up on the counter. It wasn't exact, but it looked like the way she'd last seen the books arranged.

Betty leaned in, her eyebrows raised in question. "What are you doing?"

"One more minute, Bets." She stared at the spines on the shelf, pulling one and then two books out, replacing them. She rearranged them. This was approximately how they'd looked. Satisfied, Mary brushed her hands over their spines and then looked over at her sister. "Do you remember?"

"Oh my goodness." Betty touched one of the covers and then closed her eyes, like she was struggling to find the memory. "Oh, Mary, it can't be."

FOUR

"These books" — Betty stepped closer to the counter, then glanced at Rebecca and looked back at Mary — "Mom had them."

"Exactly." Mary gave a quick clap, grateful that Betty remembered seeing them too. She waited for Betty, not wanting to rush her sister, but she sure hoped Betty had the same memory.

"They were on the shelf in her closet."

Mary smiled. That's what she'd remembered too, seeing these books lined up. Their mother, Esther Randlett Nelson, had been a lover of books, and she passed her love of reading — and collecting — down to Mary. When she was a girl, there had been books all over the house — piled on the coffee table in the living room, lined up along the mahogany bookcases with carved claw feet in the parlor, on the glass-front cabinets in Father's study. Betty and Mary each had a scuffed bookcase full of tattered Nancy

45

Drews and Bobbsey Twins. And there were always piles of novels on the table next to Mom's bed, and a whole cupboard full of cookbooks in the kitchen, and she'd even kept some books on a shelf high in her closet. Mary used to sneak in there and gaze at her mother's clothes, imagining herself wearing the long gowns she kept under plastic and the stiff dresses she starched each week before church. She would try on her mother's high heels and walk around the bedroom, then try to line them back up just right. Sometimes she would run her hands along Dad's shirts and thumb through his stack of monogrammed hand-kerchiefs, his initials DN embroidered care-fully by her mother's loving hand, but mostly, she gazed at her mother's clothes and dreamed. Mother must have known she'd done it, but she'd never let on, and Mary had loved to hide out, drinking in the air that smelled like her mother's perfume and dreaming of when she would be grown up herself. These were just like the books she'd kept on that high shelf in her closet. Betty had seen them there too.

Betty picked up one of the books, scan-ning the back cover. "That is so strange. Do you think they're Mom's books?"

Mary lifted another book, opening the

cover to see if her mother's name was inscribed on the inside. Mom had a distinctive bookplate that she placed in all her books, but it wasn't here. "I don't know," she said as she placed the book back on the counter. "I guess they could be. But it seems like an awfully big coincidence, doesn't it?"

"Mom sold most of her books," Betty said, tracing her finger along the sand in the illustration in front of her. "Before she went to live in the condo."

The familiar ache clutched Mary's heart for a moment. It had only been five years since their mother passed away, and she still missed her very much.

"Even if they are Mom's, why would they show up now, just out of the blue like that? Do you think someone is bringing them back to us?" Betty asked.

"Perhaps one of her friends was storing them?"

Mary pushed her glasses back up her nose, her mind racing through the possibilities of how these books landed on her door and who had brought them to her. There had to be a good explanation, but Mom had lived in Boston most of her adult life. Who would have her books here, in Ivy Bay? And why wouldn't they deliver the books during the day, in person? Wouldn't they at least leave a note?

"I don't know, Mary. It's pretty strange." Betty pushed the book across the counter toward her sister. "But we have other things to worry about right now." She held out the cleaning rags again. "We better get busy working."

Mary agreed and took the rags, but something in Betty's face made Mary pause. It almost looked like Betty knew something more than she was saying. But then Betty picked up a feather duster and headed for the stacks by the children's nook, and whatever it was Mary had seen had passed. She must have been imagining things. Apparently, her encounter with Karly had her suspicious of everyone.

Mary took out a rag and picked up the bottle of cleaner. Had someone brought their mother's books to her for a reason? Or were they simply a gift? Could it possibly be a coincidence? Were they even her mother's books at all?

Mary missed her husband so much at times like these. Before his death, they would talk through tough situations, trying to find a solution together. As an attorney, John had been a quick thinker, analyzing a situation quickly and clearly to determine a logical solution, or, at the very least, the next step in the process.

The only thing Mary could think to do now was obey her sister and clean. Mom would have wanted the place to be as clean and bright as possible for the visit from *Cape Cod Living.*

Mary walked toward the children's area and sprayed down the enamel sides of the tub as Betty dusted the shelves. Her sister was very busy, volunteering for a number of charities around town, and it warmed Mary's heart that Betty would take the time to help her prepare for the photo shoot.

"Hey, Bets." Mary worked on a wad of gum that clung to one of the tub's claw feet. "After Mom passed away, when you were cleaning out her apartment, did you see any of those books in her things?"

"I haven't seen those books since we were children." Betty moved the duster over the picture bookshelf as she shook her head. "I do remember finding you in Mom's closet staring at them once or twice."

"I loved to imagine what they were about." Most of the books in the house were available to Mary and Betty whenever they wanted to read them. Even their father's heavy biographies were there; all they had to do was ask. But these books, tucked away on such a high shelf, were different. She'd known in some way that they were special to their mother, that they were off-limits, and the one time she'd asked, her mother had refused, saying they were too old and delicate. She'd promised Mary she could see them when she was older, but at some point, they'd disappeared from the shelf, and Mary never asked about them again.

The door chimed, and Rebecca stood to greet Jerry Avakian, who owned Meeting House Print and Copy. He liked old-fashioned hard-boiled noir, and Rebecca pointed out a couple of new titles that she thought he'd enjoy.

Mary scooted to the other side of the tub and saw her sister on her knees, pushing the duster into the far corners of the lowest shelf. Betty seemed to be doing fine today, but Mary always worried about her sister's rheumatoid arthritis. Strenuous activity often set it off. "I'll take care of that. Why don't you go pick out flowers for the shop?" she asked.

"I'd love to." Betty straightened up and laid the feather duster down on a shelf. "What kind of flowers do you think would look good?"

"You're the flower expert." Mary shrugged. "You choose."

Betty took her tailored coat from the back

room and wrapped her violet and tan scarf around her neck, then headed toward Tanaka Florist and Garden Center.

Jerry approached the counter, a Dashiell Hammett in hand. After all that, he'd gone for one of his old favorites. Rebecca was busy shelving some of the books at the back of the store, so Mary slipped back toward the counter and moved the row of books she'd seen on her mother's shelf out of the way so she could ring up Jerry. After he paid for his book, Mary reached for one of the old books and opened the cover gently. She'd assumed that these books were worth a lot when she was a girl, that that was why Mother had kept them out of her reach, but now that she was the owner of a bookshop, she realized they were probably not as valuable as she'd once thought. The mysteries might bring two or three dollars each at her bookstore, but only if someone really wanted them. Today, someone would probably buy them more to display their beautiful covers than anything.

Jerry walked out, and the smell of baking cupcakes floated into the store.

Mary took a deep breath as she put the book back in the box. Those cupcakes smelled delicious. Her stomach rumbled, and she realized it had been a while since she'd eaten. It was too early for a cupcake, but perhaps she should go get a snack from the Tea Shoppe as she mulled over her questions. Mary knew there was little nutritional difference between a pastry and a cupcake, but it felt different somehow. "Would you like something from the Tea Shoppe?" she asked Rebecca.

"Oh no," Rebecca replied, her fingers clicking on the keyboard. "I was up half the night making cookies for Ashley's school play tomorrow night, and I sampled way too much of the dough."

"How fun!" Mary smiled at the thought of the girl who had become like a granddaughter to her performing on stage. "What role did she get?"

"She's the duck in *Click, Clack, Moo.*"

"Oh, she'll be an adorable duck."

"That's what I think too." Rebecca grinned, pushing her sleeves up over her elbows. "Would you like to come see our little duck?"

"Of course." Mary loved playing grandmother to this smart and funny seven-year-old. Being part of Ashley's young life helped make it easier to be so far away from her three grandchildren Daisy, Luke, and Emma. And enjoying a production of *Click, Clack, Moo* would be the perfect conclusion to a busy day with the magazine interview and photo shoot.

Rebecca nodded down at the row of books on the counter. "Are you ready for me to put those in the system?"

Mary glanced at them again. "I don't think so."

Rebecca tapped the keyboard again. "You're not going to sell them, are you?"

"Not until I find out if they were my mother's." Even if these books weren't owned by her mother, the reminder of Mom was there. She wasn't sure she could ever let them go.

"If you don't want to sell them, we should probably put them away so no one will think they're for sale. If you want, I can put them behind the counter for you as soon as I finish this stack." Rebecca gestured at the books she was entering into the computer.

"That would be great." Mary picked up the empty box with the tissue paper and carried that to the back room. As she set the box down, her eye caught on the green-and-pink-striped tissue paper that had been wrapped around the books. It was nice paper, and the color combination looked very modern. Mary examined it more closely. It looked the sort of paper you'd get tucked into a shopping bag at a fancy boutique. It didn't seem like something that had been stored with the books all these years. She smoothed the paper out, then started to fold it, but she noticed a sticker on the back of the paper. She flipped it over and looked at it. It looked like it had been used to seal the paper around something once, and it showed a yellow cupcake with pink frosting against a mint-green background. It was pretty, and it didn't do much to help her cupcake craving, but it was an odd thing to find with the box of old books.

Mary looked the paper over carefully, but there was no marking on it or on the sticker. It didn't seem to contain any information that would help her figure out where the books came from, but Mary didn't want to throw it out until she'd at least looked into it. She carefully ripped off the sticker, then folded the tissue paper and put it on a cabinet in the back room.

She then grabbed her light jacket for her walk to the Tea Shoppe. Betty would be hungry soon too, so she would buy a pastry for the two of them to split. She ducked behind the counter to grab her purse from its cubby and slipped the sticker into the front pocket, and her eyes lingered on the books for a moment.

As she looked at the stack of books,

another memory surfaced. When she was seven or eight, she'd come home from school on the bus and found her mother in her bedroom, thumbing through one of them. Mom had closed the book quickly, put it back on the shelf, and closed the closet door as if Mary had caught her doing something wrong. Mary had never seen her look at those books again.

Mary reached for one of the books, the one with the lighthouse, and flipped through it. This time, something slipped from the pages and fluttered to the floor. She caught her breath. You never knew what you were going to find in an old book. Sometimes she found a bookmark, or a note about the book, or a postcard from a popular vacation destination in years gone by, like Mackinac Island or Niagara Falls. Leaning over, she picked up the piece of yellowed paper from the floor and carefully unfolded it. This wasn't a scribbled note in her hands — it was a letter. Pink flowers embellished the top of the stationery, and green ivy trailed up both sides of the page. It was dated August 8, 1944, and was addressed with simple words.

"Dearest Jacob . . ."

Her breath slipped from her as she stared at the penmanship. The handwriting was neat and flowery, with delicate ridges and flourishes. It was her mother's.

The edge of the letter was tattered, like someone had read it many times. There must have been an envelope with the letter at one time, but it was now gone. Mary stared at the letter, trying to make sense of it. How did her mother's letter get into this book? And more important, who was Jacob?

FIVE

Mary's mind raced as she scanned down to the end of the letter, where she saw the signature she knew so well: Essy.

Mary sat down on the stool behind the counter.

"What did you find?" Rebecca looked up from the computer screen.

"A letter." Mary held it out, and Rebecca scanned it quickly.

"Who's Essy?"

"My mother."

Rebecca's eyes widened, and Mary reached for another book. Were there more letters? She flipped through the pages and found another letter hidden between two pages in the back. It was addressed to Jacob as well, and it was in her mother's writing. She put the two letters in the pocket of her knit cardigan, and then began searching through the other six books. She quickly located a letter in each book. She stacked them carefully on the counter in front of her. She wanted to read them, but it felt strange to do so right here, with Rebecca so close.

"I think I'll go get that pastry." Mary pushed herself up. "Do you mind watching the store for a bit?"

"Not at all." Rebecca smiled knowingly and nodded at the letters. "Take as long as you need."

Mary slipped her jacket on, thankful once again that she'd found Rebecca. She always seemed to understand things that Mary didn't want to say.

Mary reached under her jacket and put the letters in the pocket of her cardigan and stepped out onto Main Street. The sky was the perfect autumn blue, the air crisp. It reminded Mary of the fall days of her childhood, when her mother would take her and Betty apple picking in one of the orchards around New England. Mary started toward the Tea Shoppe, but then stopped. She realized she wasn't hungry anymore. She turned and walked back down Main Street the other way, toward Albert Paddington Park. She passed the bank, and the manicured grounds of the Chadwick Inn, and then sat on the white bench at the edge of the park. The smell of smoke from a chimney mingled with the earthy, woody scent of fallen leaves. She pulled the letters from her pocket, arranging them by date to read. The first one was written in the summer of 1944.

Dearest Jacob,
Your letter arrived this morning, and I was glad to receive it. I, too, could have danced for hours more. When will you return to Ivy Bay? There will be another dance at the pavilion in two weeks. Perhaps you can come again.
Yours truly,
Essy Randlett

Mary slowly folded the letter. She'd never heard her mother mention anyone named Jacob. Who was this man who enjoyed dancing as much as her mother? He must not have been from Ivy Bay, but he apparently lived close enough to attend dances in 1944.

Maybe it wasn't that strange that her mother had had a friend Mary hadn't known about. Surely she had lots of friends she'd never mentioned to Mary. And there was nothing in this letter, really, that indicated that this Jacob had been more than a friend. She reread it quickly. Jacob could have been just a friend who had taken her to a dance. But then Mary looked again at the greeting: "Dearest Jacob." It didn't sound like something you wrote to someone who was just a friend.

In Mom's later years, they talked about her life as a teenager. Mom liked to tell her daughters about the parade where she'd met their father; she thought he was too old and too arrogant, but Dad had been smitten, and eventually, he had swept her off her feet. She told stories about sneaking out with her best friend, Tabitha, and about how exciting those heady days during the war were, when everything felt tenuous, like it could disappear at any moment. She talked about the victory garden she'd grown and the sailors who passed through Cape Cod. She even told them about the accident she'd been involved in when the car Tabitha had been driving skidded off the road late one night when they weren't supposed to be out. Mom had never hidden the fact that she'd been a bit wild; she'd hoped her impetuous mistakes would help her daughters stay on the straight and narrow.

Her mother had also talked about the early years of her marriage to Davis in Ivy Bay, when Betty and then Mary were born. They talked about the family's move to Boston for Mary's father's job. And they talked about how much they both missed

Mary's father after he'd gone home to be with the Lord in 1996. Before Dad died, Mom had talked him into taking dance lessons for the first time, and they'd spent the last decade of his life dancing together. The thought of her parents dancing the fox-trot or waltz still made Mary smile.

Mary's mother had talked about all that, but she'd never said anything about a man named Jacob. Why hadn't she?

The salty wind blew over Mary, and she tightened her scarf around her neck before she opened another letter. This one was dated December 14, 1944.

Dearest Jacob,

There is so much I want to say to you, but words only confine me. Instead of writing, I wish I were beside you, holding your hand as we talk and hearing your words in return. It's been too long since I've seen you. We will meet again next weekend, as planned, but I fear I cannot wait that long to see you.

I wish I could come to you tonight. If Adam weren't watching so closely, I would find someone to take me to you.

I wish I could come to you and never leave.

Many of the boys from my class are

going off to war. It's all everyone talks about right now. No one wants to talk about the beauty of the new winter snow or about dancing. So few even want to sing anymore.

I think my heart might break if you had to go to war. I would write to you every day. And I would pray every hour, every minute, while you were away.

So please, don't go. Stay here and dance with me. I love you.

Essy

At the bottom was a sketch of a lighthouse. It looked a lot like the sketch she'd seen on one of the old books back at the store. Her stomach tumbled as she stared at the letter and picture.

Much had changed in her mother's heart since the summer letter. Her mother was clearly in love in this second letter, writing to a man who wasn't Mary's father. Why had her mother never told her about this man? Her father, Davis, hadn't danced in 1944, at least not on US soil. He was in France, fighting for the Allied forces.

Did Betty know who Jacob was, the man to whom their mother had forever pledged her heart? Did she know that her mother once loved a man besides their father?

Mary had certainly been interested in boys back in middle school and early high school, but once she met John, her heart was forever his. John was the only man who'd ever captured her heart, and he had continued to do so for forty years. Not every woman married her high school sweetheart, but it was still strange for her to think of Mom loving anyone else but the man she married. She and Dad had seemed to grow even more in love as the years went by.

But it wasn't so hard to believe, she supposed, that her mother had loved another man before she married her father. It was even a little romantic that Mom wanted to dance with this man even as the rest of the country was worried about war. Still, it was strange to read about her mother's heart, her love for this man, in her own handwriting. She'd never found any kind of diary among her mother's things, so it was a blessing to find the treasure of these letters. But again, she wondered, Who was Jacob? What had happened? Had it just been a case of puppy love, or had something else torn them apart?

The wind blew again, colder this time. Mary tucked the letter back into her pocket and took out the next letter, on a piece of yellow stationery, dated February 1945. The next five letters were similarly themed, about dancing, the war, and how much Mom loved this man. There were references to secret meetings, carefully orchestrated plans that they had taken pains to keep anyone from finding out about. Mary wondered if this secrecy had been part of the appeal — to two teenagers, sneaking around might have seemed romantic — or if there was a reason they couldn't see each other openly. The last letter was written in October of 1946, more than two years after her mother's first letter.

Dearest Jacob,

I cannot sleep. I cannot eat. I feel sick all the time. I cannot believe what we have done, and what has happened because of it. Our lives will never be the same.

I thought that what we were doing was all right, because it was done in love, but now that it is too late, I understand how very wrong we were.

I fear what will happen when they find out, but we cannot hide it for long. I should confess and get it over with, but I don't yet dare. Perhaps I shall go away for a while. Perhaps they will send me away.

I need you here beside me. I need your strong arms around me. When will I see you again? I can face sharing our horrible secret if I have you here with me.

I am confused as ever, but my feelings for you have not changed.

My heart is forever yours,

Essy

Mary sat still, stunned. In the other letters, her mother had sounded like a teenage girl in love. Here, she sounded like a young woman in trouble. In a specific kind of trouble. But surely her mother wouldn't have —

Mary read the letter again, slowly, examining every word. It couldn't mean what it seemed to. She checked the date on the letter again. October 15, 1946. But that didn't make sense. Esther Randlett had married Mary's father in early December, 1946. Had her feelings for Jacob changed so quickly that she had fallen in love with Dad that fast? Or was it possible that . . .

Mary leaned back against the bench. The wood felt cold and hard under her.

Betty had been born in June of 1947. Eight-and-a-half months after that letter to Jacob.

It could only mean one thing. Yet surely not. Was Betty Jacob's child?

Six

Mary was still sitting on the bench, staring at nothing, trying to work through what she'd just read, when her cell phone rang. She didn't know how long she'd been sitting there, but it had grown chilly, and she zipped up her jacket and pulled her phone out of her purse. She looked down and saw Betty's number. She tried to figure out what to say to her sister, but Betty started talking as soon as Mary answered the phone.

"It took me forever to pick out the flowers I wanted," Betty said, talking quickly. "But I have dozens of beautiful roses and lilies in my backseat."

It took a moment for the words to register. Then she remembered — the store, the flowers, *Cape Cod Living.* Mary slipped the letter back into the pocket of her cardigan. "They sound beautiful."

The wind swayed the branches again. "I can't wait to show you. I just got back to the store. Are you coming back soon?"

"Yes, I'll head back now," Mary said.

"Great. I'll see you in a minute," Betty chirped, and Mary hung up the phone. But she sat there for a few more minutes, trying to figure out what to do. Should she tell Betty what she suspected? Should she look for proof? What if she had read it wrong? Maybe there was some other explanation for the strange letter?

Mary wasn't sure, but as she pushed herself up off the bench, she decided that she was going to find out.

The branches of the maple trees glistened in the sun as Mary walked back up the lane, and she could see that they were beautiful, but she didn't feel the same rush of thankfulness and joy the leaves usually inspired in her. She tried to think about what she needed to do to get ready for the photo shoot tomorrow, but the excitement of the *Cape Cod Living* feature was now overshadowed by the discovery of these letters.

Except, she realized, she didn't really discover the letters. Someone brought them to her. Whoever dropped them off must know something about them. She would have to figure out who brought the letters and find out. Whoever that person was, there was a good chance he or she would know about Jacob and could answer the questions now swirling in her head. She would also need to figure out a way to broach the subject of Jacob with Betty. How could she figure out if it was true? Did she really want to know? Would what she found out change anything between the sisters?

Mary thought about her mother. Esther had always been something of a free spirit, as well as warm, confident, and artistic, unafraid to express her feelings. She loved gardening and always had dozens of different kinds of flowers blooming in the yard, and each summer, they ate vegetables grown from her garden. She could see some of the young girl dancing under the stars in the woman her mother had become. But Mom had also been strict with her daughters, keeping close tabs on their comings and goings and making sure she knew who they were with at all times. Mary had always chalked it up to good parenting. But was she extra vigilant because she knew what could happen if her daughters weren't careful?

Mary headed toward Meeting House Road and walked by Ivy Bay Bank & Trust. As she was passing the front door, her good friend Henry Woodrow opened it from the inside, waving toward the clerk as he stepped onto the sidewalk. He was wearing a flannel shirt and khaki pants. Even though when Mary had first moved back to Ivy Bay they hadn't seen each other in decades, it was almost as if no time had passed at all. He was just as good a friend now as he had been over forty years ago.

Henry had been nothing but a gentleman to her since she'd returned to Ivy Bay, a confidant for her, and even a bit of a cheer-leader. He didn't flinch when she told him about John, just as she listened to him talk about how much he missed his wife, Misty. These days, she found herself relying more and more on his company and listening ear.

Henry continued backing toward her, still chatting with the clerk, his silver hair glinting in the sun. Laughing, Mary lifted her hands to his back to stop him from running into her. He whirled around, surprise flooding his sea-green eyes. "Are you trying to flatten me?" she asked.

He laughed. "I'm so sorry!"

She put her hands into her pockets, checking to make sure the letters were still there. "I don't think I've sustained any injuries."

"Why don't we start over?" He released the door and tipped his baseball cap to greet her. "It's a pleasure to see you, Mary Nelson

Fisher. How are you on this fine, windy day?"

She hesitated. She wanted to tell him about the letters but not on the street like this. "I'm all right." He nodded, and she continued before he could ask any more questions. "It's a beautiful day."

"It's spectacular, isn't it?" He glanced at his watch. "Have you had lunch?"

"I haven't, but —" she began. It was hard to believe it was just lunchtime. So much had already happened this morning. But she had to get to the shop now. Not only was Betty waiting for her to set out the flowers, but she also wanted to talk to Betty about the letters. She didn't think she'd be able to focus on anything else until she had. "It's a busy day."

"Now, that's what I was afraid of." His warm grin grew even larger. There was kindness there, just like there had been in their younger years. "I thought you might get yourself so busy with work in your book-shop that you'd forget to eat. And as it turns out, I just booked a large group that wants a private tour of Cape Cod Bay on my boat next week, and they've just given me the deposit. So I was hoping for a celebratory lunch, anyway."

She smiled at him, knowing that he was

exactly right. Between her reading and working, she'd been skipping too many meals recently. "I'd love that. And it has been busy. But I can't right now."

"In an hour, then. We could meet for lunch at the Black & White Diner." He gestured to the diner down the street, which was already hopping with the lunch crowd. "We'll eat fast."

She moved her fingers over the letters one more time. It would be good to talk to Henry, about both the letters and the magazine story. "Sure. Lunch sounds great."

"Does one o'clock work?"

Wind gusted up the street again, and she shivered. "One would be perfect."

Henry put his hand on her elbow, nudging her forward. "In the meantime, you need to get out of this cold."

She said good-bye and walked toward the bookshop. It was good to have Henry to count on when she needed a friend. The sweet aroma of fresh flowers greeted Mary when she walked into the bookshop. There was already a floral bouquet on the front table, and Betty was arranging a vase of flowers on the round table in their reading nook. Rays of sun drifted through the bay window, and the bouquet of burgundy roses and butterscotch lilies lit the room.

"What do you think of these flowers?" Rebecca pointed back at one of the three fresh bouquets that decorated the shop. "Didn't your sister do an amazing job? I can't get over those arrangements."

Betty shook her head. "You're exaggerating."

Mary hung up her coat and admired the warmth that the flowers added to the store, especially the cozy reading area. "She's right, Bets. You're an artist."

Her sister smiled. "I'm glad you like them."

"I love them," Mary said, stepping closer to examine her sister's work. "What do we need to do next?"

"I was going to work on the window display." Betty pointed to the yards of fluffy white fleece and cans of white spray snow she'd purchased and left on the counter.

Mary started to pull down the paper leaves of the autumn display. "I'll help."

Rebecca picked up her coffee mug and hopped off the stool. "How can I help?"

"Actually, do you want to break for lunch?" Mary suggested. "I have lunch plans in a bit, so maybe now is a good time."

"Are you sure?"

Mary nodded. "This way, you can take your break before I leave and not starve to death waiting for me to return."

Rebecca grabbed her denim jacket from the back room. "Gotcha. Then I think I'll head down to the marina."

Mary nodded. Rebecca was a writer, and she often spent her lunch breaks writing in an old fisherman's shanty by the water.

"I'll be back soon," Rebecca said as she opened the door. The sound of the chimes above the door mixed with her words.

Mary went to the back of the shop and turned on the gas fireplace. The scent of the roses sweetened the reading area. She sat down on one of the twill chairs in front of the hearth and called for Betty to join her. "I have something to show you."

Betty crossed the room, and Mary set the stack of letters on the small table between the chairs. Betty sat across from her and smoothed her pants. "Who are these from?"

"I found them in the books that were delivered last night." Mary inched the letters across the table.

Betty looked at Mary curiously as she reached for the top letter, and her jaw dropped when she scanned the page. "These were — They were in those books?"

At Mary's nod, Betty picked up the next letter, and then the next. Mary waited patiently for her to get to the last one. When

Betty finished the last letter, she set it back on the stack and stared at the flames dancing in the hearth before them.

Betty handed her the letters. Mary held them in her lap, as if having them close to her would help her understand a bit more about her mother. She waited for Betty to say something, but her sister didn't speak. The only sound was the crackling of the flames in the fireplace behind them.

"What are you thinking, Bets?" There were spots of color on Betty's cheeks. Betty had always been thinner, more fine-boned than Mary. And Betty's hair had always been lighter, a pale honey-blonde, not like Mary's coarser brown hair; nothing at all like Mom's wild dark curls. Dad had also had dark hair, and he used to joke that the milkman was the only explanation for Betty's light hair and fine features. Mary had always chalked these differences up to the wonders of genetics. But could there actually have been different genes involved the whole time?

Betty gave a slight nod of her head, her gaze on the fire. "I think this can't possibly mean what you seem to think it suggests."

Mary understood her sister's reluctance to accept the implication, and she wanted to agree with Betty, but what else could that letter possibly refer to?

"I know it's a lot to take in, but do you think —"

"No, I don't." Betty said it so quickly that Mary was taken aback. Her sister was usually so calm and put together, and this news had clearly rattled her.

"But the timing is pretty convincing. Mom always said you were premature, but what if —"

"No, Mary." Betty picked at an invisible piece of lint off her pant leg. "I was born small, just like any preemie would be. I had to stay in the hospital for weeks before they'd let me come home." Betty had always had health problems, even from birth, when she had been diagnosed with jaundice and had to be monitored carefully in the hospital nursery. And she had been much smaller than Mary at birth, and, honestly, ever since, but different genetics could account for that. "It's just not true. Mom would have told me."

"But she didn't tell anyone about Jacob. She wouldn't have —"

"She told me."

It was Mary's turn to be speechless.

"She told you about Jacob?" she finally managed to sputter.

"Yes." Betty continued to pull at her pant

leg. "A few weeks before she died. I was reading to her — this was back when she'd gotten really weak — and she asked me to put the book down, and she just started talking. She was reminiscing about high school, and all the good times with Tabitha, and then she started talking about her first love, a man named Jacob."

Mary tried to absorb this news.

"And you never told me?"

"I didn't think it was my place. I also didn't think it mattered. I thought it was just a sweet story about a first love."

"Why didn't *Mom* tell me about him?" Mary had always considered her mother a close friend; she couldn't deny that it hurt to hear that she had chosen to share the story with Betty and not her.

Gus walked out of the back room and hopped onto Mary's lap. She scratched him behind his ear as she fought to untangle the thread of envy that wove itself around her heart. Even if she didn't talk about him much, why had their mother chosen to tell Betty about this man and not her? She knew it wasn't Betty's fault that Mom told her, but she wished that her mother told her as well. The verse she'd memorized from James 3:16 filled her mind. *For where you have envy and selfish ambition, there you find disorder and every evil practice.* There was no room for envy in her heart or her mind. It would only wedge a gulf between her and Betty, and like the Scriptures said, bring disorder in their relationship instead of kindness and contentment. She and her mother, in their quiet times of talking and walking together, had discussed many things. For some reason, her mother had chosen not to speak about Jacob with her.

Mary smoothed the top of the letters. "What did she tell you about Jacob?"

Betty shrugged. "Only that she met someone named Jacob while she was in high school. Someone she wasn't supposed to love."

"Do you know what she meant by that?"

Betty's fingers went to the simple strand of pearls around her neck, and she straightened the necklace. "Do you remember much about Grandfather Franklin?" Betty was the history buff in the family, and she had always paid a lot more attention to the family tree.

"A little bit." Grandfather Franklin had died when she was nine, and her mind wandered back to the years before his death. Adam Franklin, her mother's stepfather, had been the mayor of Ivy Bay. The town had adored him, even memorializing him

77

with a small statue at the library. He fought for his town and the people in it. At home, he expected perfection from his stepdaughter Essy, and later, from his grandchildren. Even though she was young when she visited the Franklin home, Mary remembered how uncomfortable she'd felt, like she shouldn't speak or touch anything or even breathe except when absolutely necessary.

On the other hand, just a mile or so away, her father's parents — Gram and Gramps Nelson — had welcomed her and Betty into their home with joy, asking them questions and playing games with them when she and Betty were children. She'd loved her summers with Gram and Gramps Nelson. She didn't remember one time that she'd felt uncomfortable in their house.

"Grandfather Franklin wasn't an easy man to live with," Betty continued. "And Mom said he was very particular about the boys that she spent time with."

Mary stretched her feet out in front of her. The warmth from the fireplace felt nice. She wasn't cold in the shop, but the heat on her skin awakened her mind to think. The amount of information she was trying to assimilate in such a short time was overwhelming.

"That's understandable. It's good that he was cautious about the boys Mom dated," Mary said. She and John had certainly been careful about who they allowed Lizzie to date when she was in high school. Maybe their mother had fallen in love with a man who wasn't good for her.

"Of course Grandfather should protect her, but I'm afraid he was more concerned about his image than Mom's well-being. Mom told me that he wanted her to marry a man who could help establish his reputation and political career. Jacob was poor. Apparently, his father was a fisherman. According to Mom, Jacob wasn't good enough for Mom in Grandpa Franklin's eyes." Betty shook her head.

Mary knew that Grandfather Franklin had run twice for state senate in the 1940s — and failed twice. While the town of Ivy Bay loved him, it seemed he couldn't generate enough votes outside the town's limits. She could understand how a match between his stepdaughter and an influential man might have helped his political career.

Mary straightened the pile of letters in her lap, and she felt a bit of sadness for her mother, thinking about her being forced to marry for Grandfather Franklin's career instead of marrying a man she loved.

No. Her mother *had* loved her father. Long after Grandfather passed away, her parents had been inseparable.

For a moment, the only noise was the crackling of the flames in the fireplace.

"Mom told me all that," Betty finally said, her voice quiet. "If Jacob were really my father, she would have told me that part too."

Mary thought about that for a moment.

"But, Betty, why would she have told you and not me about Jacob at all? Why would she do that unless it was something she wanted you in particular to know?"

"I don't know, Mary." Betty pulled at her pant leg. "She was just talking. She probably didn't even know what she was saying. But this letter" — she pointed at the stack in Mary's lap — "it must be about something else. You of all people know that old saying about not judging a book by its cover."

"But what if it's not about something else?" Mary said gingerly, leaning forward in her chair. "Bets, what if Jacob *was* your real father?" An hour ago, Mary wouldn't have believed it could be possible, but now, given all that she'd learned, it sounded entirely plausible.

Betty shook her head, an indignant look

on her face. "Mom is gone, and we don't know who this Jacob is. I don't see how we'd ever find that out." Betty adjusted the sea-green pillow behind her and leaned back against the cushions.

From the hard set of her jaw, Mary could see that Betty's mind was made up. And Mary could understand Betty's hesitation. The idea that the man you'd always known and loved as your father might not have been biological — that your mother had lied to you your entire life — these were hard to swallow.

But Mary couldn't just leave it alone. This mystery had landed on her doorstep — literally — and now somehow her whole family history might have been a lie. If she didn't find the truth, she'd always wonder.

"Betty, someone out there knows the truth. Someone left those books and the letters for me to find. I'm going to try to find out what happened to Jacob."

"Or maybe" — Betty crossed her legs and looked Mary in the eye — "this is one mystery you should leave alone."

SEVEN

The smell of bacon wafted into the street when Mary opened the door to the Black & White Diner. It had been a staple on Main Street for decades, and locals flocked here for breakfast — especially their chocolate-chip pancakes — and lunch all year. Henry was already seated at a booth in the corner, chatting with Nicole Hancock, the head server, as she refilled his glass of iced tea. Nicole's blonde hair was swept up in a messy knot, and she wore turquoise earrings that matched the color of her eyes. Her family had owned the diner for generations, and her father was now the cook, so Nicole had grown up here and knew all the locals' favorite orders.

"How are you?" Mary asked as she gave Nicole a quick hug. Then she flung her purse into the booth and scooted in across from Henry.

"Just fine, thank you."

Henry's eyes twinkled. "Nicole was just telling me her son has discovered a passion for Lincoln Logs."

Nicole laughed. "The problem is, he doesn't want to build with them." Without breaking eye contact with Mary, Nicole grabbed a glass from a drink stand behind her, poured Mary a glass of iced tea, and slid it in front of Mary. "He hides them all over the house and gives me clues on how to find them."

Mary loved to hear Henry's laugh. "Perhaps he will be a mystery writer someday," she said.

Nicole tapped the menus in her hand on the table. "Or maybe he will solve the mysteries like you do."

Mary laughed with both of them as Nicole handed both her and Henry menus. It felt odd to her that people identified her as a detective of sorts. She didn't try and find mysteries, yet they kept falling into her lap, begging to be resolved.

Mary started to open the menu, even though she had it memorized. Sometimes, seeing all the options made her want to try something she hadn't eaten in a while.

"Dad wants me to tell you that the special today is fresh mackerel." She tipped her head slightly toward Henry. "I won't name any names, but someone we both know just caught it this morning."

Henry laughed. He was up before the sun most mornings and supplied a good number of the restaurants in town with a fresh catch every day.

"Now, how can I refuse freshly caught mackerel?" Mary sipped the drink. "I'll take that."

"Good choice." Nicole nodded and made a note on her little pad. "And the burger for you, Henry?"

"Can you put some bacon and cheese on it?" he said, grinning like a schoolboy.

"Of course." Nicole took the menus with a grin. "That'll be up in just a minute." She ducked behind the counter and disappeared into the kitchen.

Mary took a sip of her iced tea. It was cool and refreshing. Just what she needed.

"So you said you booked a big tour?" Mary said, looking across the table at Henry. He ran a fishing business with his boat *Misty Horizon,* but he often did special group tours around the bay.

Henry smiled, and the lines around his eyes crinkled. He was tan from all the time he spent on his boat, and the sun left silver highlights in his hair. "A wedding party. They wanted a sunset cruise after the rehearsal dinner. You know what weddings cost these days."

Mary knew Henry would never charge a group more just because it was a wedding, but she also knew that families often didn't skimp on the services they were willing to pay for to impress their wedding guests. Henry was no doubt making a tidy sum from the event.

"So what has got you so busy today?" he asked as he ripped open a packet of sugar from the dish on the edge of the table. The ice in his glass tinkled as he stirred it in with his straw.

Mary sighed. "I don't know where to begin."

"How about at the beginning?" He cocked an eyebrow, and Mary had to smile. Talking to Henry always did make her feel better.

"First of all, *Cape Cod Living* is sending a writer and a photographer to the bookshop tomorrow. They're going to write a feature on the store."

"That's the best kind of news, Mary. People will come from all over to visit your shop." He leaned forward, whispering like he was proposing some sort of conspiracy. "You let me know if they want to go fishing while they're here."

She laughed. "If they want to go fishing,

I'll make sure to send them your way."

"So you have a magazine editor coming to write about you," Henry said. "That's exciting and all, but there's something else going on, isn't there?"

It always surprised her that he could read her so easily.

"I had the oddest thing happen last night." She twisted the cold glass in her hands. "Someone delivered a box of books to the shop, long after I closed. This morning, when I was going through the books, I found something in them."

His eyes widened. She loved that he could be just as curious as she was. "What did you find?"

She lowered her voice. "There was a letter hidden in each one of them."

One of his eyebrows slid up as he studied her. "How do you know someone was trying to hide the letters?"

The heat turned on in the vent above them, blowing warm air over their table. "Good question. I suppose I don't know for certain, but they were tucked between pages in the back of books."

He gave a small shrug. "Maybe someone just found a unique way of storing their correspondence."

"Yes, but these weren't just any letters."

86

She paused, taking a sip of her iced tea. "These were written by my mother."

He sat back against the booth, looking as surprised by the news as she felt. "Your mother?"

She nodded. "To a man named Jacob."

He cleared his throat, lowering his voice as well. "A man she liked?"

She sighed, looking back down at her glass. "Very much."

"Before or after —"

She cut him off. "Before my parents were married."

"Well, hello there, Mary." Mary turned and saw Lori Stone sidling up to the table. "Henry, how nice to see you." Lori was the Realtor who had sold Mary her shop, and she was friendly and outgoing. And even though Lori had chosen a somewhat awkward moment to enter the conversation, this is what Mary liked about living in a small town — you ran into your neighbors everywhere you went.

Henry nodded, and Mary smiled and said, "Hello, Lori. How are you?"

"Oh, you know, it's the slow season." She shrugged. "But I found out this morning that the Rivers Accounting firm over on Liberty will be closing, so there will be another storefront to fill. So that's something." Mary knew that Lori didn't mean to sound callous. A business closing wasn't something to be glad about, even if it did mean a potential commission for Lori. But in the late fall months, she was probably grateful for any new listings. "But, hey, I couldn't help but overhear you saying *Cape Cod Living* is going to feature your store."

Mary nodded proudly but was a little concerned that Lori had overheard their conversation. Had Mary been talking that loudly?

"That will be such great publicity for our little town. And I just wanted to say that if they need any information about Ivy Bay, please feel free to send them my way. I'd be happy to help them however I can."

Mary nodded. Lori did know a lot about Ivy Bay and was good at talking up its finer points. Mary had witnessed that firsthand. But she realized she'd been so focused on preparing her shop for the interview that she hadn't stopped to consider how this story might benefit all the businesses in Ivy Bay. It was about more than just her bookshop. The story was about bringing more people into Ivy Bay, and places like the Black & White Diner, Sweet Susan's Bakery, and Gems and Antiques would certainly get a bump from the article too. Business in Ivy

Bay was slow for everyone this time of year, and they would no doubt appreciate any help Mary could send their way.

"I'll do that," Mary said, giving Lori a smile. "Thanks for offering."

"Anytime." She looked down at her watch. "Oh, I have to run. I'm showing a couple some houses for their retirement this afternoon. Fingers crossed." With that, she hurried away, and Mary smiled, watching her go.

Nicole stepped up to the table, a plate balanced on each arm. Nicole slid Henry's burger in front of him, and a perfectly grilled and seasoned filet of mackerel before her.

"Compliments to the chef," Mary told Nicole. Then she nodded back at Henry. "And compliments to the person who caught such a fine piece of meat."

"The fish were begging me to catch them this morning." He took a bite of his bacon cheeseburger and flashed her a thumbs-up sign. Mary had to laugh. If you covered an old shoe with that much bacon and cheese, it would taste good. She broke off a bite of the fish. It was as fresh as promised, and even more delicious than she'd anticipated.

"So, what do you know about this Jacob?" Henry asked, returning to the conversation they'd been having before Lori interrupted them. And even though it seemed like a non sequitur, Mary followed, and they picked up their conversation right where they left off.

"Not much," Mary admitted, lowering her voice. "Only that he apparently wasn't good enough for Grandpa Franklin but Mom apparently loved him. And —" She hesitated. Did she really want to spread this around when she wasn't sure if it was true? Henry brushed his fingers off with a napkin and waited expectantly.

She was being silly. This was Henry. He wasn't going to tell anyone. She let her voice grow even quieter. "And one of the letters hinted that my mother might have been pregnant before she met my father."

"Oh, Mary." He shook his head. "I don't know. Your mother was a good woman."

"Good women make mistakes," Mary said. "It happens all the time."

The edge of a paper napkin fluttered in the warm air from the vent above them.

"If it was true, that would mean . . ." His voice trailed off, like he couldn't bring himself to finish his thought.

"That he was Betty's father." He shook his head, but Mary continued. "It's possible. The timing works out."

"Well, if you really want to know if it's true, there's an easy way to find out."

Mary poked at her fish with the tines of her fork, waiting.

"You could do a DNA test. If Betty is your full sister, your DNA should match hers. And if it doesn't" — he paused, like he was trying to figure out what to say — "well, at least you'll know."

Mary laid down her fork. It wasn't a bad idea. These things were probably done all the time. She wasn't sure how she'd get Betty to agree, but it was worth asking. "How did you get to be so smart?" she asked.

Henry returned a broad smile. "Many years of practice."

When Mary returned to the bookshop, Betty had gone home and Rebecca was helping a woman with two young children navigate the children's nook. Rebecca's daughter Ashley was there too, pointing out her recommendations. Ashley came over after school most days, and Mary often joked that they should put her on the payroll, since she was probably their best salesperson. There was only one other customer in the store, a young man in his late teens whose face was buried in a book.

Mary asked him if he needed help, but he politely waved her away and turned his attention back to the book. Mary grinned. She understood his wanting to continue reading without interruption. Once she started reading a good book, she was usually wrapped up in it. Gus was sleeping in a patch of sunlight that streamed in through the front window. She wouldn't mind a nap herself, but she had too many things she still wanted to get done today.

Mary hung up her coat, then sat down behind the counter and pulled an Ivy Bay phone book out from one of the cubbies. She had her mom's best friend Tabitha's number at home, but it shouldn't be hard to find it now. She flipped to the residential listings, and then ran her finger down the column of *K* names. Krause, T. Mary reached for the phone and tried to think of what she would say as she dialed. How could she casually ask her mother's friend if Mom had secretly had a child out of wedlock and lied about it for the rest of her life? Mary prayed that God would give her the words to say.

Dawn, the woman who had cared for Tabitha for almost a decade, answered the phone.

"Hi, Dawn, it's Mary Fisher. Is Tabitha home?"

"How are you, Mrs. Fisher?" Dawn asked. Dawn was unfailingly cheerful, and she always seemed to be glad to hear from Mary. Mary was sure her upbeat attitude helped keep Tabitha in good spirits as well.

"Oh, I'm just fine. Thank you," Mary said. "How are you doing?"

"Just great. It's a beautiful day." Mary could hear classical music playing on the other end of the phone.

"Is Tabitha free?" Mary asked.

"I'm sorry, Mary. Tabitha is home now, but she's taking a short rest. I hate to disturb her, but I know she'd love to talk to you. What can I tell her this is regarding?"

Mary wasn't sure how much to say over the phone, but she also wanted to be sure Tabitha understood her urgency. "I got a box of books with some strange letters my mom wrote when she was young, and I would really love to talk to Tabitha about them."

"I see. Are you free later?"

"Of course. What would be a good time to call back?"

Mary watched as the young man put the book back on the shelf and turned to go. Mary waved as he walked out the door.

93

She'd prefer that people not come in and read her books without buying, but maybe he hadn't found the story as interesting as he'd first thought. She still needed to be gracious if she wanted repeat customers.

"Instead of calling back, why don't you come on over and visit?" Dawn said. "She doesn't get many visitors these days, and I know Tabitha would love to see you." Mary knew Dawn wasn't trying to make her feel guilty, and it would be nice to catch up with her mother's friend in person.

Mary eyed the clock. It was now mid-afternoon, and she'd been gone from the shop a good part of the day. "Could I come over around six, after I close the shop?"

"That should work just fine," Dawn said. "Seeing a friend does her body and soul good."

Mary hung up the phone and turned to look at the stack of her mother's books sitting behind the counter. Ashley led the woman and the kids to the register, assuring them they would be pleased with their purchases, then settled into the bathtub to go over her lines for the school play. As Rebecca rang up the woman, Mary bent down and picked up one of the books. How were they connected to the letters, and to her mother's history? She flipped through the pages, searching for any markings or scribbled names. All she needed was an address or name or another thread of a clue to go on — anything she'd missed. The books were all different genres. They were all written by different authors. The only thing that tied them together, as far as Mary could tell, was the similar illustrations on each of them. It seemed a fair assumption that the same artist had worked on each of the covers. Was the artist somehow connected to the letters? Mary looked at the book in her hand again. It was the first one she'd seen, with the boy building a sand castle on the beach. She checked the dust jacket, and then flipped the book open to look at the copyright page. There was no mention of the artist who worked on the covers. She closed the book and drummed her fingers on the counter. How could she find out more?

The woman and her children opened the door, and the bell chimed as they stepped out. The noise woke Gus, who stretched lazily and pushed himself up. He sat up and stared at Mary, as if he was waiting for her to do something.

"Was the store busy while I was out?" Mary asked as Rebecca shut the drawer on the old-fashioned cash register.

"Not too bad," Rebecca answered, turning to the computer. She typed something on the keyboard. Mary looked and saw that she was entering information into their inventory software. "Sandra Rink came in and got the next book in that baking mystery series you got her hooked on."

Mary nodded. Sandra was a teller at the bank, and she had told Mary she didn't read much until Mary gave her a copy of a cozy mystery series she suspected Sandra would like. Sandra was now blowing through the series at such a quick pace Mary would probably need to order copies of the later books in the series soon. Giving Sandra that first copy free had definitely paid off, just as it often did.

"And Mr. Engle came in and bought another Tom Clancy book," Ashley called from the children's area. She was lying in the bathtub, her legs draped over the side, studying what looked like a page of a script. She didn't even look up.

"That's right." Rebecca nodded. "And a woman came in and tried to buy that stack of books you got last night."

Mary halted. "Really?" How had someone even known about the books? She supposed it was possible that someone other than Lori Stone had overheard her talking with Henry at the diner. Mary wasn't sure she'd ever get used to how quickly news traveled in a small town. "Was she from Ivy Bay?"

"I don't know, but I've never seen her before. She seemed a little nervous, though, and almost secretive when she asked about the books. There was no need to whisper, since there wasn't another soul in the shop while she was here."

Gus rubbed up against Mary's feet, and she bent down and scratched between his ears. "What did she look like?"

"She was in her early twenties, I'd say. Very sophisticated, with long black hair and green eyes."

"That's strange," Mary said. That must be the same young woman who was here this morning, searching for a job. Karly Sundin. She'd seemed to recognize the books then; if she'd tried to buy them, it confirmed Mary's suspicion.

"I know who you're talking about. Her name is Karly. I met her earlier and showed her the books. She acted strange, but she didn't offer to buy them then. I wonder what made her change her mind."

Rebecca shrugged. "Maybe she just likes really old books."

Mary put her fists on her waist. "They're not *that* old," she teased. Rebecca laughed, but Mary's mind was whirring. What did Karly want with these books? What did she know about them? Mary decided she needed to track her down and find out. Maybe she could stop by Gems and Antiques before she went to Tabitha's and see if Karly had made it there to talk with Jayne.

Mary turned back to the book in front of her, but Gus meowed and hopped up in her lap, so she set it down and stroked the cat's soft fur. "Have I been ignoring you today, Gus?" Mary said, and Rebecca laughed. Okay, so maybe Gus was a little bit spoiled. But what was the fun of having a cat if you couldn't spoil it rotten? Gus was such a fixture in the store sometimes people came in just to see him and ended up buying books. He certainly earned his keep.

She looked back at the book. How could she figure out who the cover artist was?

The telephone by the register rang, and Rebecca answered it. "Mary's Mystery Bookshop. How can I help you?" She paused. "Sure, she's right here."

Mary glanced up at her as Rebecca pushed the Hold button and held out the phone to her. "It's Harrison Greer. From *Cape Cod Living.*"

Mary cleared her throat and answered the

call. "Hello, Harrison. Nice to hear from you."

"Hi, Mary." Harrison's voice was just as rushed as when he'd called early this morning. "Unfortunately, I have some bad news."

Mary felt her heart begin to sink. "Oh?"

"My photographer has to go to Martha's Vineyard in the morning to take pictures for another story, so I'm afraid we won't be able to come your way after all."

She sighed. The story would have been good not only for her, but as Lori said, it would have been good publicity for all of Ivy Bay. Betty and Rebecca would be just as disappointed with the news.

"It's all right," she relented. What else could she say?

Harrison barked an order to someone in the background before he came back on the phone. "Can the photographer and I come on Friday instead, at ten?"

Her heart picked back up again. "You still want to come?"

"Of course. We still want to feature you in January."

"That would be fine." When she hung up the phone, Rebecca began typing on her keyboard quickly. Mary grinned and put her elbows on the counter. "You don't have to pretend you're working."

Rebecca let out a sigh of relief, and Ashley pushed herself up in the bathtub. "What did he say?" Ashley called.

"They're coming to do the story on Friday instead."

"That's okay, isn't it?" Rebecca said.

Mary nodded. She was relieved, actually. She'd been excited about the story, but also feeling a little overwhelmed about getting ready, especially since she was so distracted by her mother's letters. Now she could spend the next two days searching for information about Jacob instead of worrying about preparing the shop for a photo shoot.

"I'll just have to tell Betty. She'll probably want to get some more flowers so they're fresh on Friday."

Gus walked around on her lap. He kneaded her leg, getting ready to settle in for a while, and then started pawing at the edge of her long cardigan. She patted him absently, her mind returning to the problem of the artist.

"Ouch. Gus, stop." Mary picked the cat up and moved him to a different spot on her lap where he couldn't knead her stomach, but he moved right back to the same spot and started poking at her pocket. "Gus, no," she said. She heard papers crinkle and fished the letters out to keep them from being mangled by the little cat's paws. As she set them on the counter, the top letter fell open, and Mary's eyes fell on the drawing of the lighthouse at the bottom.

If she didn't have Gus in her hands, she would have smacked her forehead. How could she have missed it before? The drawing was done in pen, and the cover artwork was watercolor, but now that she saw the book and the sketch next to each other, it was clear that they had both been done with the same delicate strokes. They were clearly by the same person.

Mary looked again at the lighthouse sketch. She didn't know how the letters had ended up in the books, but she did know that there was one person who'd had the letters in his possession at one point. Someone who had spent enough time in Ivy Bay to draw a convincing representation of the old lighthouse both here and on the cover of the mystery novel.

Mary had a strong suspicion she knew just who had painted these book covers.

EIGHT

After Rebecca and Ashley left for the night, Mary flipped the Open/Shut sign on the shop door to Shut, secured her mother's letters in her pocket, and stepped out onto Main Street. She'd come back and get Gus on her way home. She walked across the street and looked in the front window of Gems and Antiques, but the lights were out and the front door locked. She'd have to stop by earlier in the day tomorrow and try to catch Jayne. She walked to Meeting House Road, where her car was parked at the curb in front of Cape Cod Togs, and headed out to Tabitha's. She turned right onto Pheasant Lane and passed through one of her favorite neighborhoods in Ivy Bay. Some of the most charming and oldest homes on the Cape were tucked back among the trees here, where Tabitha lived, most of them built in the 1800s. Some were the traditional New England saltbox homes, while others were two-story gabled homes with wide porches and bay windows. Each house embodied the history of the town in their clapboards and shutters, and they were surrounded by gardens that reminded her of pictures she'd seen of old English gardens.

She loved this neighborhood, especially because it was the same area in which her mother had spent much of her childhood. She drove slowly down the street where her grandparents had lived. Mary parked in front of the brick colonial where her mother had grown up and where Mary had spent so much time in her childhood. Mary climbed out of the car and looked at the familiar house, with its nine windows on its front and a large chimney that rose on the left side. An enclosed walkway on the right led to what had once been a kitchen. A wall of river rocks wove in front of the house, trailing out into the surrounding woods.

Behind the house was a rocky brook and a wooden bridge where Mary used to play when she was a girl, throwing sticks and leaves into the water and watching them float away. Mom's bedroom had been on the side of the house, facing the trees, and she used to tell Betty and Mary about her escapades into the forest when she was a girl.

Mary knew that her mother's childhood hadn't been especially happy. Essy was the youngest of three children, and her father had died when she was young. Mary Randlett, suddenly a young widow, took in sewing to make money, but during the worst years of the Depression, times had been lean. But then, Mary married again to Adam Franklin, a successful attorney in Ivy Bay who later became mayor. Adam, as Mary had been reminded earlier today, had had aspirations and expected his family to act a certain way and make him look good. Mom had never given any indication that he'd been cruel, but, then, the letters Mary had read today had shown that he'd certainly exerted control over Essy's life.

The house had been sold out of the family years ago, after Grandpa Franklin died, back when Mary was just a child. The current owner would certainly have cleaned the house top to bottom multiple times since then, and likely would have trashed or given away anything the Franklin family left behind. But it wouldn't hurt to at least check, Mary decided. It was possible the current owners found the books in a box of her family's things and by chance decided to bring it to the bookshop Mary happened to own. It was a long shot, but since she was here, why not ask?

Mary started toward the front door when a woman carrying a toddler stepped outside and walked toward the minivan parked in the driveway. The woman met her eye. "Can I help you?"

"I have kind of a strange question," Mary said, laughing sheepishly. "My mother used to live in this house, and I was taking a little stroll down memory lane."

The woman opened the car door and started buckling her son into a car seat inside. "We love the house. We've been so blessed to be here." She straightened up and waited for Mary to go on. Her brown hair was pulled back into a neat ponytail, and she was wearing dark jeans and a brown turtleneck under her wool coat.

"I own the new bookshop on Main Street, and I received a box of books last night. You didn't happen to find the box in your house and bring them to me, did you?"

The woman shook her head. "I'm sorry. We just bought the house a couple of years ago, and everything was cleaned out when we moved in."

"I figured," Mary replied. "I just wanted to check. Thanks, anyway."

Mary didn't linger. If the books hadn't been discovered in the Franklins' old house, there wasn't much more she could learn here. But hopefully, Tabitha would have some answers.

Tabitha's house was only a few doors down, and it was one of the newer homes in the neighborhood, Mary knew. It was a grand house, built in the Queen Anne style, with gingerbread trim, a cupola, and a wraparound porch.

Mary eyed the top windows of Tabitha Krause's two-story home. There were a lot of stairs for an elderly woman to manage, but Mary was glad that instead of moving to a retirement community, Tabitha had been able to remain in her home with Dawn's loyal assistance. Tabitha had three children, but her granddaughter was the only relative who remained in Ivy Bay. Amelia Shepard lived across town with her husband, Jimmy, the owner of Jimmy's Hardware, and Mary knew she came to see Tabitha regularly.

Mary lifted the iron knocker and pounded twice on the door that had been painted a light purple color. Seconds later, Dawn opened the door.

"Hello, Mary," Dawn said, gesturing for her to step inside. Dawn was a dark-skinned woman with an easy smile and a slender build. "I'm so glad you could make it. Tabitha just finished dinner a few minutes ago, and she is going to be so excited to see you."

Mary stepped into the foyer and marveled at the grand staircase made of intricately carved dark wood. It was polished to a high sheen, and the crimson runner that snaked up the middle of the steps was plush and clean. The soft beige walls and the oil paintings warmed up the space that could have felt imposing and overwhelming. Mary had been here before, many times, but unlike most places, this didn't look any smaller than it had when she was a child.

"You wait right here. I'll go get Tabitha," Dawn said as she walked down a hallway and disappeared into a room that branched off to the right.

Mom had always come to see Tabitha when she brought the family to the Cape when Mary and Betty were young. Mary remembered many lazy days on the beach with her mom and Tabitha. Mary and Betty would play with Tabitha's three kids, chasing crabs and building sand castles and digging for the buried pirate treasure they were sure was just under the sand, while Mom and Tabitha chatted and laughed. When Mary was very young, she had thought Tabitha was her aunt, until Betty had informed her that she wasn't related by blood. Tabitha had a hard time getting around these days, but she'd shown up at some events in Mary's store, and Mary had made a point of seeing her regularly since she'd come back to town.

Dawn stepped back out into the hallway and walked toward Mary, but she seemed to be looking past her.

"I'm sorry, Mary," Dawn said quietly. She rubbed her finger and her thumb together and kept her eyes on the floor. "I didn't realize that Tabitha was asleep."

"Oh." Mary started. That was strange. Only a minute ago, she'd just finished dinner. "But I thought you said —"

"I was mistaken." She said it gently, but firmly. "I'm sorry."

Mary tried to read her face, but Dawn wouldn't look at her.

"Do you think she'll be asleep long? I could wait if it's just a quick nap. I'd really love to talk to her."

"I'm sorry, she's asleep." Dawn glanced back down the hallway, as if she was looking for something, and then turned back to Mary. "And I don't know how long she'll be out. I'm afraid this is not a good time."

Mary glanced at her watch. It was only

6:20 pm. "Perhaps I can come visit her tomorrow?"

"Maybe," Dawn said, and she opened the door. She gave Mary a weak smile, and, just barely, shook her head.

As Mary walked back to her car, she couldn't help but think Dawn had been as confused as she was about why Tabitha couldn't see her tonight. Was Tabitha avoiding her?

Mary stopped at the shop and coaxed Gus into his carrying case before she began her short drive home. She also slipped a couple of her mother's books into her purse in case she had a hard time sleeping again and wanted to look through them. She was disappointed that she hadn't been able to speak with Tabitha tonight, but she would try again tomorrow. Maybe Tabitha really was resting. Perhaps it had nothing to do with avoiding Mary. She was quite elderly, after all. She needed sleep.

Darkness was settling over Ivy Bay, and the streetlamps gave a subtle light to the village. Mary drove slowly down Main Street. Sweet Susan's was dark, and she could see Sophie Mershon moving around inside the Tea Shoppe, getting the store ready to close for the night. She passed Bailey's Ice Cream

Shop — another one of her favorite places in Ivy Bay. Every month, they featured one of Mary's ice-cream recipes that she concocted in her kitchen and then handed over to the ice-cream shop to make for their customers. This month's flavor was Pumpkin Cream. Her mouth watered just thinking about it.

As she drove home, she thought about what she would say to Betty. Mary knew her sister had been surprised by what Mary had suggested, and not exactly thrilled with the idea, and she hoped that Betty wasn't upset with her for bringing it up. She would need time — they would both need time — to come to grips with the idea. Betty hadn't come back to the shop this afternoon, but the shop had been mostly ready for the photo shoot when she'd left, and Mary knew Betty had things to do.

As she turned onto Shore Drive, an odd thought crept into her mind. Was it possible that Betty was the one who'd kept Mom's books, that she had been the one to leave them anonymously on Mary's door? She'd called Mary on her cell phone last night, asking when she was going to be home. Was it possible that Betty had been calling to see where Mary was at the time? If she had dropped off the books, why would she do it secretly, and so long after Mary had been in Ivy Bay?

Mary shook her head. Betty had been so surprised by the letters. She couldn't have faked that reaction. It was possible, Mary supposed, that she hadn't known that the letters were inside the books, but that seemed unlikely.

Mary opened the front door. After she released Gus from his case, she took off her coat and scarf and put them in a closet by the door. Betty was in the kitchen, pulling a pan of lasagna out of the oven.

"Hello. How was your afternoon?" Mary said tentatively.

Betty sighed and set the pan on a pretty tile trivet. She was stiff, but not like when her arthritis flared up. "It was okay," she said simply.

The air hung heavy. Mary decided to just come out and address the elephant in the room.

"Bets, I'm sorry. I know those letters were difficult to read." Mary stepped into the kitchen and walked toward her sister, ready to wrap her in a hug, but Betty waved her away. Mary looked around and tried to figure out what she could do to help. The table needed to be set. That would give her something to do. She opened the cabinet next to the sink and took out two plates and set them on the well-worn wooden table, on opposite sides of the glass vase filled with purple asters and golden chrysanthemums from Betty's garden.

"It's not your fault, Mary. I know that." Betty grabbed the pepper mill, and she ground fresh black pepper over the simmering cheese sauce. "I know what that letter made it look like. But Mom had to be talking about something else. I know it isn't what you think."

Mary nodded. She wasn't so sure, but even if the letter had been referring to some other secret her mother had kept, she wanted to know what it was.

"It's speculation at this point," Mary said, mostly to reassure her sister. She set out glasses and then took down the glass pitcher and held it under the faucet. Clear, cool water splashed into the bottom. "But I am trying to find answers." Betty started to protest, so Mary kept talking. "Hopefully, we'll find out that it's not true. But there seemed to be an easy way to find out, so I stopped by Tabitha's house tonight to see what she could tell me."

Betty pulled a fresh green salad in a wooden bowl out of the fridge and set it on the table. "Good. She knew Mom back then. She told you it was crazy, right?" She dug around in a drawer and then pulled out a wooden spoon and fork and set them in the bowl.

"Actually, no."

Betty's spine straightened.

"She wouldn't see me."

"That doesn't sound like Tabitha." Betty leaned back against the counter and crossed her arms over her chest.

"I thought it was strange too. And it made me suspicious."

Betty raised an eyebrow. "Suspicious of Tabitha?"

"Suspicious that she knows something she doesn't want me to find out. She could have been the one who dropped those books off last night for me to find."

"Mar, she can hardly walk without help." Betty slid oven mitts over her hands and lifted the lasagna off the counter.

"She could have found someone to do it for her."

"But if she wanted you to find the books and the letters, why not just give them to you? Why leave them anonymously? And why avoid you tonight? It doesn't make any sense."

Mary had to agree that it didn't make sense. But decades of reading mysteries had taught Mary that just because something didn't make sense, it didn't mean there wasn't truth buried somewhere in it. She'd have to keep looking.

"Henry suggested another way we could find out for sure."

Betty moved toward the table, holding the lasagna out in front of her. "What's that?"

"We could get a DNA test."

"No." She set the lasagna down with a *thunk.* "That's not necessary. Asking Mom's old friend to shed some light on the letters is one thing, but a DNA test is — well, it's crazy." Betty grabbed the back of a chair, as if for support.

"But what if it's true?" Mary spoke softly. "Wouldn't you want to know?"

Betty watched her, and then she slowly pulled out her chair and sat.

"I don't see how it could possibly matter one way or the other." Betty began to serve herself from the hot dish. When she'd cut a piece for herself and scooped it onto her plate, she nodded at Mary. "May I serve you?"

Her message was clear. The conversation was over. Slowly, Mary lowered herself down to her chair. She hated that she'd hurt Betty. She hadn't meant to, but she could see that Betty was upset. And as curious as she was, nothing she could find out would be worth alienating her sister.

"Okay, let's forget about the DNA test," she said. "I'm sorry."

Betty nodded and then bowed her head to bless the food. When they dug into the steaming plates of rich, cheesy lasagna, things felt a little less tense.

"This is delicious," Mary said. Betty used spicy sausage and roasted mushrooms to give the lasagna a hearty flavor, and it tasted especially good tonight after the cool fall day.

They ate in silence for a few minutes, but the tension had gone out of the air.

"So are you ready for the big shoot tomorrow?" Betty finally asked. Mary appreciated that she was trying to change the subject but felt bad that she'd been so caught up with the books and the letters that she'd forgotten to tell her sister that the shoot had been rescheduled. Betty took the news in stride and volunteered to get some new flowers Friday morning to spruce up the bunches she'd bought today. Mary asked more about the church food drive, and Betty told her about the shelter they planned to donate the cans to, but Mary's mind kept drifting back to the letters and to Jacob. If she could find out where the letters came from, that would probably lead her to someone who knew what really happened. But how?

She'd have to find out more about Karly Sundin, for starters. And she'd try to get in touch again with Tabitha. Mary tried to remember what she'd learned about genetics in high school biology. She had blue eyes, her mother had green eyes, and her father had brown. Betty had blue eyes too. She thought blue eyes from brown and green was possible but unlikely; could it have happened twice to the same parents? She'd have to do some research. If she could get a DNA test done, that would be the simplest, but if Betty wouldn't agree yet, that would have to wait.

If she wanted to, Mary could easily take a piece of hair from her sister's hairbrush or take a glass she'd drunk from to a lab without her sister's permission, but that was not honest, and she wouldn't do that to her sister. And more than anything, she didn't want to let her imagination run away with her. Just because the letters seemed to suggest the unthinkable didn't mean it was true. Mary didn't want to make something out of nothing.

Then again, it wasn't "nothing." Too many strange things had happened within the past twenty-four hours to ignore. The box of books, the letters, Tabitha's avoidance. She was not imagining things.

She needed to try to find out more about Jacob. She knew only the vaguest details — not even a last name — from the letters, but she'd see what she could find out. There had to be some record of the man — a marriage announcement, property transfer, death certificate — in the public record. She'd start by seeing what she could find at the library first thing tomorrow. And she'd try to find out more about the art on the book covers. Mary had a strong suspicion that Jacob had done the art for the covers. Maybe she could find information from the publisher that would lead her to Jacob.

Mary sighed. She didn't have a lot to go on. If only Mom had left them more information.

Betty was now talking about gathering volunteers to take the food to the shelter, but Mary had just realized something. What if there was more? If this Jacob had been all that important to Mom, wouldn't she have kept more than just a few old letters and books?

"What happened to all of Mom's things?"

Betty looked startled, and Mary realized she'd just made it obvious that she hadn't been listening to Betty.

"I'm so sorry, Betty. I am interested, really."

Betty gave a tentative nod that made it clear she didn't believe her.

"I'm so glad Bernice volunteered to help you take the food to the shelter." Mary had picked up that much of what Betty was saying, and it was enough to get a reluctant nod from Betty. "But I just realized that Mom might have had more information about Jacob that we just never saw. There might be something in all that stuff we cleared out of her condo."

Betty laid down her fork. "It's upstairs, but I went through it all when she died, and there's nothing about Jacob in those boxes."

Mary and Betty had worked together to deal with Mom's things when she passed away, but Betty had handled boxing up most of her things and selling the furniture, while Mary had focused on the logistics of selling the condo and making funeral and burial arrangements. Betty no doubt had gone through Mom's things much more carefully than she had, but it was still worth taking a look.

"After dinner, could you show me where the boxes are?"

Betty hesitated. "Do you really want to do

this, Mary?"

Again, for just a moment, she wondered why Betty was hesitating. Did she know more than she was letting on? Was that why she didn't want Mary looking into this?

But then Mary looked at the set of her sister's lips and the almost fearful look in her eyes, and she dismissed the idea. If she found out that Jacob really was Betty's father, it would change Betty's whole life. Of course she was nervous.

"We may find something that clears it all up," Mary said. "Something that shows that I was reading that letter all wrong."

Betty laid down her fork and took a sip from her glass. She looked at Mary, then down at her plate and back to Mary.

"After dinner, I'll show you where the boxes are," she said at last.

After they finished their meal, Betty rinsed off the dishes and Mary put them into the dishwasher, and then they headed upstairs. Mary pulled a cord from the ceiling in the second-floor hallway, and a set of wooden stairs unfolded onto the floor. Mary went up into the attic first and turned on the lights. The walls were unfinished, and the raw boards and light carpet made the room feel open even though it was piled with cardboard boxes and plastic bins. Betty had years' worth of her own family's things up here, as well as Mom's and Dad's stuff, and things from her husband, Edward, and his family. Mary had even stored some of her stuff here when she'd moved in with Betty.

Betty pointed to the far left corner, by the dormer window. "Mom's boxes are over there."

She pointed to four plastic boxes, about two-by-three feet each, stacked against the wall. The top one was light enough for Mary to lift, and she put it on the floor between them. She sat down on a cardboard box, and she gestured for Betty to do the same. Slowly, Betty joined her. Mary opened the lid of the box, and she pulled out a few old bridal magazines and a couple of paperback books. She flipped through them, but the art was not at all like on the other books, and there was nothing between the pages. She pulled out a faded leather photo album, and she slowly turned the pages. There was a picture of her parents' wedding at Grace Church. Her father was wearing a dark gray suit and striped bow tie, smiling at his bride with obvious affection, but Mom was looking off toward something behind the camera. She wore a long cream-colored gown with a high, pleated waist, her wild dark hair twisted up into a demure chignon. The dress was beautiful, but — Mary leaned in, trying to get a better view of the waist.

It was the height of fashion in the later 1940s, she knew. But that style could have easily hidden an expanding waistline.

"Can I see that?" Betty asked, leaning in to look, and Mary moved the book so she could see it. Betty looked at the photo, then pressed her lips together and turned the page without saying a word. Mary scooted her box closer to Betty's and looked over her shoulder as she flipped to photos of Betty as a newborn and then a toddler. Mom and Dad had been loving parents, and they had loved each other; that much came through in the photos. But that didn't answer her questions.

There were envelopes full of Mary's and Betty's old art projects and progress reports, as well as programs from church concerts and old birthday cards. Mary could have spent hours looking through all this, but she tried to focus. She was looking for anything that referred to Jacob.

Betty reached for another photo album while Mary retrieved an oval jewelry box. It was satin white, with faux pearls glued to look like ribbons along the top and front. The jewelry box had been on her mother's dresser when Mary was a girl, and often, when Mom opened it, Mary would hover over her shoulder to look at the sparkling contents. Mary smiled as she remembered how her mother had let her go through the necklaces and brooches when she was a child, treating each like they were pieces from the crown jewels. All of Mom's real gems had been divided between Mary, Betty, and Mary's daughter, Lizzie, according to the will, but there were several pretty costume pieces laid out on the white satin lining, including a faux-pearl necklace and a good imitation ruby ring. She set the jewelry box down and reached in the container again. All that was left was some old clothes. Mary pulled out a fur stole, a pillbox hat, a pair of stained white satin gloves, and a gray silk A-line dress wrapped in white tissue paper.

"Can you believe Mom fit into this dress once?" Mary asked, holding it up. The dress was knee-length and cut slim, and made for someone quite small. The fabric shimmered softly in the light from the naked overhead bulb.

Betty looked up from the photo album. "It's hard to believe anyone ever could. But, then, Mom had quite the figure back when she was young."

"I wonder if Daisy would ever wear this,"

Mary said, referring to her sixteen-year-old granddaughter. She stood and held it up in front of her. Daisy was slim, but it might not be her taste. Still, it might be worth asking her. She shook the dress gently, and something fell out of the lining.

She picked up the bundle and straightened up. It was a white linen handkerchief, wrapped around something heavy.

"Was this here when you packed up these clothes?" Mary asked.

"I don't know. I didn't go through the clothes all that carefully," Betty admitted. "They were in a pile in her closet, and I put the whole stack in the box to sort out later."

Mary unknotted the handkerchief and pulled out a bracelet. It was silver and had dozens of small crystals mixed with what looked like emeralds inlaid in the silver. She held it up to the light, and the prisms made a rainbow of colors dance across the boxes.

Mary held it out to Betty. "Look at this. I never saw this when we were children."

Betty looked down at the unique piece of jewelry. "I don't remember seeing it either. It's pretty."

"But why isn't it with the rest of her jewelry?" Mary asked.

Betty shook her head. "Mary, I could be wrong, but this looks real. Look at how the light refracts," she said, pointing to prisms that scattered over the floor as the bracelet moved. "I think those are real diamonds."

"They can't be," Mary said, leaning in closer to examine the bracelet. "Why would it be sitting up here if it were real? Why wasn't it mentioned in the will like all the rest of her good jewelry?"

"*If* it's real. I don't know," Betty said. "But I bet the Tuckers could help you figure out if the stones are just good fakes or they're actually genuine."

"Good idea." Mary set the handkerchief and bracelet aside. Had Dad given her the jewelry for an anniversary? How had it ended up with the old dress, which she would have had to have been quite young to wear? Jacob came to mind, but she didn't say it out loud.

"Look at this," Betty said, and gestured for Mary to lean in and take a look at the photo album in her hands. "This is an album of Mom's from her high school years."

Mary moved closer to look over Betty's shoulder. On the first page was a black-and-white photo of her mother in the long pleated skirt and sweater of her cheerleading uniform.

Mary turned the page and saw picture

after picture of Mom and Tabitha at the beach, cheering side by side, and leaning against the hood of a classic Cadillac. It was apparent that they were the best of friends. If anyone remembered the man who'd caught her mom's attention in high school, she was certain Tabitha would.

Betty turned the page, and Mary's eyes widened. It was a photo of their mother on the beach. She was wearing a demure skirted swimsuit, not like the skimpy things girls wore these days, and big sunglasses. One of her hands was lifting a hat in the air, and her other hand . . . it was holding the hand of a handsome young man. A man who was clearly not her father. His hair was light, and he was thin, with delicate bone structure, and very handsome. Her mother was smiling radiantly at him. The two of them looked happy, like they belonged together.

"This is Jacob." Mary didn't have any evidence, but somehow she knew.

"Perhaps," Betty said, but her eyes didn't leave the picture. Mary gave her a moment, then carefully reached over and edged the photograph out of the squares that had probably held it for almost seventy years. There were no names written on the back of the photo, but there was a date. August

1945. The time her mother had been writing her letters to Jacob.

She handed it back to Betty, who continued to gaze at it. She couldn't seem to look away.

NINE

The next morning, Mary arrived at the Ivy Bay Public Library five minutes before it opened. Dark clouds were building on the horizon, and the air was a few degrees cooler than it had been yesterday, but it hadn't started raining. It wouldn't be too many weeks before snow filled Ivy Bay's backyards and iced the ponds. She wore khaki pants, a burgundy-and-navy-blue knit sweater over her navy-blue turtleneck, and a fleece jacket, but even with all her layers, she shivered from the cold.

Victoria Pickerton laughed as she climbed out of her car and saw her friend waiting outside the brick building.

"Another mystery?" the librarian asked. Victoria had helped Mary find answers to several questions in the past, and she was always game for whatever strange request Mary brought her way.

"Of sorts," Mary said, and smiled guiltily

as Victoria unlocked the building's white front doors. The head librarian wore a deep-blue tunic over gray leggings and pink cat's-eye glasses that Mary thought might look unusual on most people but looked just perfect on Victoria.

As Mary followed Victoria toward the main desk, she glanced at four bronze sculptures lined up on the wall. One of the sculptures was of Grandfather Franklin, and it perfectly captured his stern face, spectacles, and his wavy hair that tucked behind his ears. She didn't often think about her grandfather's influence on their town, but Mom once told her that this library wouldn't exist — or at least not in such a well-preserved building — without his doggedness. He'd spearheaded the effort to landmark important buildings, and now the historical society had designated several dozen buildings in Ivy Bay as landmarks. No matter what she found out about her family, or what she remembered from childhood, she was grateful to her grandfather for many things, including his determination to protect and preserve his town's heritage.

Weak light stole through the skylights in the library's tall ceilings and reflected off the blonde oak of the bookshelves and desks. Mary inhaled deeply. She loved the way libraries smelled.

"So what can I help you find today?" Victoria asked as she sat down behind the front counter.

"I'm looking for some information on a man named Jacob."

"Does Jacob have a last name?" Victoria asked with a smirk. She'd worked with Mary enough to know that Mary had done a lot with less than that.

"Probably." Mary smiled. "But darned if I know what it is."

"Does Jacob live in Ivy Bay?" Victoria asked.

"I have no idea. He didn't in 1946, which is the last date I have for him."

"You do like to make things challenging, don't you?"

"I like to keep you guessing."

"I'm guessing, all right. Without a last name or any other information, I don't know what to tell you. I guess you could start with the old issues of the *Ivy Bay Bugle.*"

Mary nodded. "I was thinking I'd scan through them and see if anything pops up."

"You know where the machines are," Victoria said, gesturing toward the archive room. "Have at it. And good luck."

Mary walked to the archive room and settled down in front of one of the old microfilm readers. Many libraries with bigger budgets had gone digital, but Mary thought there was something charming about seeing the actual newspaper pages on the old microfilm. Unfortunately, it was a slow process. As the machine warmed up, Mary went to the drawers and took out spools that had back issues of the *Ivy Bay Bugle* from the mid-1940s. Mary threaded the first roll, which started in 1943, into the machine, and started scanning. She wasn't sure what she was looking for exactly but hoped she'd find something.

Mary read headlines about the war. There were profiles of local women who grew victory gardens and announcements about scrap-metal drives. There were beautiful advertisements for furs and canned vegetables and a new dress shop opening on Main Street. But she made it through 1943 without seeing anything that caught her eye.

Mary leaned back, stretched out her neck, and reached for the next spool. She loved reading the old articles and seeing photos of what Ivy Bay looked like seventy years ago, but she was starting to lose hope. Maybe she should just give up and head to the shop. She'd find some other way to learn more about Jacob. But then, midway through 1944, she saw a story about a dance in Albert Paddington Park. Mary centered the article and enlarged it, focusing the lens carefully. The timing was right. This could have been the dance where Mom met Jacob. She scanned the text quickly. It was short; all it really said was that the USO had put on a dance in the park, and there were a couple of grainy photos of the event, but no matter how closely she looked, Mary didn't see anything — or anyone — in the pictures that looked familiar.

Mary blew out a breath and leaned back in her chair. Talk about a needle in a haystack. She glanced at her watch. It was a little after ten. Rebecca should be at the store by now, opening up. She trusted Rebecca completely, but she should still get going to help her. She'd just finish this spool and then head out.

Mary quickly scanned through the rest of the articles, but she didn't find anything that seemed helpful. She pushed herself up and stretched, and then returned the film to the drawers resolutely.

The library had filled up while she was in the archive room, and Mary smiled at the handful of toddlers playing tag in the children's area while their mothers chatted.

Better here than in her store. She headed toward the front door.

"Any luck?" Victoria called from behind the counter. She placed a receipt in a paperback romance and handed it to Nicole Hancock, who waved at Mary and headed out the door.

"Nothing," Mary said, shaking her head.

Victoria gestured for her to come closer to the counter. There was no line at the checkout desk, so Mary walked toward her friend, scooting around the kids who were now careening around the large main lobby area.

"What led to the search for Jacob?" Victoria asked as she pulled a handful of books out of the return bin and stacked them on the counter. "Maybe that will help me think of where to look."

Mary pulled the two books she'd taken from the shop last night out of her bag. "These books were left at my shop the other night."

Victoria reached out for one of the books and pulled it closer. "This cover art is beautiful," she said and adjusted her glasses to get a better look at the boy building a sand castle. "It's almost luminous."

Mary nodded. "That's sort of what I'm looking into. I think Jacob might have done the art for these covers." Mary didn't go into the letters, and she was grateful Victoria was discreet enough not to ask too many questions.

Victoria picked up the book and looked at the spine. "Hartell Press," she said, looking at the little square logo on the spine. "I think I've heard of them." She leaned back in her chair. "But they're not one of the publishers I deal with."

"I don't know anything about them," Mary said, shaking her head. She had intended to look into the publisher later. The publisher might be able to put her in touch with the artist, and that could lead her to Jacob. "Does the copyright page say anything else about them?"

Victoria held it out, and they both looked at the small type. There wasn't much information on the page, but there was an address: 183 Bleecker Street. "They're in New York," Victoria said. She laid the book down and turned to the computer screen on the counter. "Let's see what else we can find out." She typed in something on her computer and waited while it loaded.

Mary tried to be patient while Victoria skimmed through the list of hits. Victoria clicked on a link, shook her head, and clicked on something else.

"It looks like Hartell was a small family-run company. They seem to have done all different kinds of books, but mostly fiction. They had a couple of romances hit the best-seller lists in the sixties." She narrowed her eyes at the screen. "But it looks like they went out of business in the seventies," she finally said. She turned the screen so Mary could see it. It was a Wikipedia entry about the company, which, if the page was to be believed, was now defunct.

"Well, that was a bust," Mary said.

"Just because the company doesn't exist anymore doesn't mean it's a dead end," Victoria said, but Mary could see she was trying just a bit too hard to be cheerful.

"That's okay, Victoria." Mary smiled and took the book back. "I'll find some way to track down Jacob. There's got to be something out there about him."

"If there is," Victoria said just as two young moms came up to the counter, arms piled high with picture books, "I'm sure you'll find it."

Mary put the books back in her bag and stepped to the side so the women could put their books down. "I sure hope you're right."

Mary walked out of the library and headed right on Meeting House Road. She had a few more stops to make before she headed back to the bookshop. As she walked, she checked her phone to see if Dawn had called to schedule a time when she could come visit Tabitha, but there were no messages. She dialed Tabitha's number and turned onto Main Street as it rang. It rang four, five, six times, and then Tabitha's answering machine picked up. Strange. Dawn was usually there and could get to the phone if Tabitha couldn't. Mary shook her head, left a message, and slipped her phone back into her pocket.

Mary crossed Main Street to visit Gems and Antiques.

"Hi, Mary," Jayne called as Mary stepped inside. She was just setting out a set of delicate china on top of a burled oak dresser. Her auburn hair was pulled back into a low ponytail, and she was wearing khakis and a blue button-down shirt. "Looking for anything special today?" Jayne bent down and pulled a dish wrapped in tissue paper from the cardboard box at her feet and started to unwrap it.

Mary laughed. "Yes, in fact. And I found it. I was looking for you."

"Well, fancy that." Jayne pulled a teacup out of the paper and set it gently on top of a stack of plates. It was a lovely pattern of pink roses and graceful greenery, and Mary knew Betty would love it. She'd have to remember to mention it to her sister. "And here I was going to track you down today to thank you for sending Karly my way." She nodded toward the back of the store, past china dolls, trays of silver, old cradles, and an ornate pewter mirror, where Karly was bent over the jewelry case with a young male customer.

"I take it that means you hired her." Mary watched the girl.

"I did. When she showed up here yesterday, I just had a feeling about her. And I was right. She is a born saleswoman." She took another dish from the box and lowered her voice. "That guy is ring shopping. If he doesn't walk out of here with an engagement ring, I'll be shocked."

Mary's eyes widened. "Not a bad first sale." Jayne and Rich stocked a wide selection of vintage jewelry from many different eras, but it was all high quality and came with a price tag to match. Selling an engagement ring would bring in quite a bit of money. Mary glanced back at the girl, but she was leaning over the case, pointing out different options to the young man, who looked a bit overwhelmed. Karly looked up and gave Mary a nervous smile, then turned back to the display case.

"Oh, it won't be her first sale," Jayne said, tapping the dresser. "She sold this piece to a couple yesterday afternoon."

"Very nice." It was a gorgeous dresser, with intricately carved drawer fronts and clawed feet, and what looked like original mother-of-pearl hardware. Mary eyed the price tag affixed to the corner of the piece. It wasn't cheap either.

"Did you find out much about her in your interview?" Mary was fishing, but thankfully Jayne didn't seem to notice.

"Oh, we didn't interview her." Jayne waved away Mary's question. "Rich and I both chatted with her for a bit, and I knew I liked her, so I asked her to start immediately."

"How nice. Do you know where she's from?"

Jayne shook her head. "You know, I don't. I do know that she lives with her grandfather." Jayne pulled another teacup from the tissue paper and held it up to the light. Then she wiped away a smudge with her finger and set it next to the other one. "But I suppose that's all I really know so far." She laughed at herself, without a hint of distrust at her instincts.

Mary knew Karly would have had to have filled out a W-2 if she wanted to get paid, and that would have her address on it, but she certainly couldn't ask Jayne for that. If someone had asked her about Rebecca's financial information, she would never have given it out. But Karly might be forthcoming with information if Mary just asked.

"If you don't mind, I'd love to chat with her when she's done with the customer. Do you know how long she might be?"

"Hard to say." Jayne straightened up. "They've been there for a while, but it is a big purchase, so who knows? With an engagement ring, you want to make sure you get it right."

"I do understand that." Mary looked down at the pearl ring John had given her on their tenth anniversary. She'd learned afterward how much time and energy he'd spent picking out just the right piece. It had been absolutely worth it. The ring was priceless to Mary.

"But I'll let her know you want to speak with her," Jayne offered. "I could have her come by your shop a little later."

"I would appreciate it," Mary replied. Mary had several questions for Karly. Hopefully Karly would be ready to be honest with her.

"There was one more thing I wanted to ask you about," Mary said and looked around to make sure no one else was listening. As soon as she did it, she realized how silly it was, since there was no one else beside Karly and the young man in the shop, but for some reason, she didn't want Karly to overhear. She reached into her purse and pulled out an envelope and slid the bracelet she'd found yesterday out into her hand. She held the bracelet out to Jayne. The gems caught the overhead light and sent prisms onto the dresser. "Can you tell me anything about this?"

Jayne took the bracelet out of Mary's hand and held it up to eye level. She looked it over carefully, then turned it over and examined the back side. "Where did you get this?"

Mary wasn't sure exactly how to answer that. "It belonged to my mother," she said. That was the simplest answer.

"It's beautiful," Jayne said. Mary tried to read Jayne's face, but Jayne was squinting, and she couldn't tell if that was a good sign or a bad one. "Let me grab Rich. He'll be able to tell you more," Jayne said, and carried the bracelet with her to the back of the store and disappeared into the back room. Mary knew that Rich loved gemstones, while Jayne was the antiques expert, so it made sense that she would want to get his take on it. A minute later, Rich followed Jayne out onto the main floor of the shop carrying the bracelet. His hair was shaved down to the skin, and he was wearing a neatly pressed shirt and a tailored suit jacket with jeans.

"Good to see you, Mary," he said, smiling broadly. Rich didn't spend as much time on the floor of the shop as Jayne did, and he was less outgoing than his wife, and with his large build and shaved head, some people were put off by him, but Rich had a warm voice and was always welcoming. "This is gorgeous. Where did you say you found it again?"

"It was in my mother's things in the attic," she said. "Betty and I found it last night."

Mary glanced over at Karly and saw that she was still talking to the young man, seemingly oblivious to the conversation they were having at this end of the shop.

Rich let out a low whistle. "Just laying around in an attic. I'm always amazed when that happens. There are probably small fortunes stuffed up into attics all over Cape Cod, and nobody even knows about them."

"So it's worth something?"

Rich held the bracelet up to the light. "I'd have to examine it much more closely to

140

give you a definite value, but yes, I'd guess it's worth a lot. If there are no flaws in these stones, you could be talking about a down payment on a house."

Mary was stunned. "Are you sure?"

"Again, I'd have to take a closer look to be sure. Would you like me to have it officially appraised?"

"No, that's not necessary," Mary said, shaking her head. If it was worth anything like what he said it was, it raised even more questions than she'd had before. What was her mother doing with such a valuable piece of jewelry tucked away in her old things? Had she inherited it from Adam Franklin's side of the family? If so, why wasn't this in a safe-deposit box somewhere, or with her other valuable jewelry, or why hadn't she sold it? Mary's parents had never been poor, but they weren't well-off either, and if her mother had somehow inherited such a valuable piece of jewelry, they were practical enough to have sold it, or at least protect it. And it should have been mentioned in her will.

"If you change your mind, let me know," Rich said, handing it back. "And I'd be very careful with it if I were you."

"Thank you." Mary slipped it into a pocket on the inside of her purse. She had to talk to Betty about this. They might look into a safe-deposit box, at least until they figured out what to do with it. "I really appreciate your help."

Rich waved and headed back into the rear of the shop, and Jayne assured Mary that she'd send Karly her way. Mary walked out of the shop, trying to wrap her head around what she'd heard. As Mary walked back to her shop, she tried to think through all the possible explanations for why her mother had this piece of jewelry, but she came up short. She was going to need more information. She'd have to keep digging.

Mary decided she had time to make one more stop before she headed to the bookstore. She ducked into Sweet Susan's and inhaled deeply as the door closed behind her. Susan had decorated the store in a warm, enticing shade of butter yellow. The shop smelled delicious, like baking bread and sweet frosting. Mary's stomach rumbled.

"Hey, there," Susan Crosby called as Mary entered. She held a chocolate cupcake in one hand and a knife smeared with yellow frosting in the other. She had a yellow apron tied around her waist, and her brown hair was pulled back into a neat ponytail. "How are you today?" Susan was as sweet as the treats she sold, and the way she somehow smiled with her whole face — her eyes as well as her mouth — made everyone feel welcome in her shop.

"I'm doing well," Mary said, eyeing the selection of treats laid out on the display case. Flaky croissants were nestled next to *pain au chocolat* and hearty scones. Crumby, fluffy muffins were piled in baskets with neat little hand-printed signs that announced today's flavors: blueberry crumble, lemon poppy seed, mixed berry, and frosted pumpkin spice. There were also fresh loaves of crusty bread, as well as glistening fruit pies, and there were half a dozen varieties of cookies in pretty glass jars on top of the case. Mary checked out the cupcakes, piled high with fluffy frosting in a variety of pastel colors. Mary didn't know what Susan put in that frosting, but it was heavenly, and the cupcakes looked as good as they tasted.

Susan saw Mary eyeing the cupcakes. "I just set those out. There's chocolate, lemon, pistachio, red velvet —"

Mary held up her hands. "Don't tempt me. I need a few more walks on the beach and far fewer cupcakes." But they really did look delicious. There was a vanilla with light blue frosting the same color as the sky on a winter afternoon that was calling to her.

"Well, what did you come into a bakery for if you weren't looking for temptation?" Susan laughed like someone who had fallen to temptation a time or two herself.

"I actually wanted to ask you a question," Mary said. "Do you have a second?"

Susan put down her knife and the cupcake she was holding and wiped her hands on her apron. "For one of my best customers? Always." She winked, and Mary felt heat creep up her cheeks. Maybe she did come in here more often than she liked to admit.

Mary pulled the cupcake sticker out of her purse and held it out across the display case. "Do you recognize this?"

Susan studied it carefully, narrowing her eyes, bringing it close to her face. Finally, she looked up at Mary. "It looks like a cupcake to me," she said.

Mary laughed. "It's a good thing I got an expert's opinion on that one."

"Where is this from?" Susan asked, looking at it again.

"That's what I'm trying to find out," Mary said. "I was wondering if you recognized the logo."

Susan shook her head and handed the sticker back to Mary. "It looks like something you'd see in one of the gourmet bakeries in Beacon Hill. But I don't recognize it."

Mary glanced at the sticker again and then tucked it into her purse. "Well, it was worth a shot," she said.

"Sorry I couldn't be more help," Susan said.

"That's okay," Mary said, and she slung her purse over her shoulder and started for the door, but her eye caught on the blue-frosted cupcake again. She could almost taste the sweet, buttery frosting.

"Did I forget to mention we're having a half-off sale on blue cupcakes right now?" Susan said, nodding at the display case.

"You did forget to mention that. That seems like quite a specific sale."

"But convenient. How can you pass that up?"

"Okay, you win," Mary said, relenting. "I'll split it with Betty."

"Sure you will." Susan handed the cupcake to Mary and waved as Mary headed out the door. "See you soon!" she called.

When Mary finally slipped inside the bookshop, Rebecca was busy helping a customer. Mary gave Rebecca a quick wave, thankful once again for her capable employee, who could be counted on to cover for Mary when she was out looking into a mystery. She put her purse in the cubbyhole behind the counter and pulled out the Hartell books.

There had to be some connection between Jacob and the publisher. If they had used his art on so many of their titles, they must have known him well. She turned to the computer, which Rebecca had booted up when she came in, and typed the words "Hartell Press" into Google. She came across the same Wikipedia page Victoria was reading from in the library. Mary skimmed it again but didn't learn anything new. She clicked back and looked at the other results. There were some used books for sale that listed Hartell as the publisher, but nothing that gave her any new information. She tried "Hartell Press Jacob," but the results just got further off the mark.

Rebecca stepped up to the counter to ring up her customer, and Mary closed out of the window and paged through the book, looking for some clue that she had missed. There had to be something in here that could lead her to Jacob.

"Still thinking about those books, huh?" Rebecca said as the customer left the store. She reached for the one that was still lying on the counter, opened the cover, and started flipping through the pages of that one.

Mary sighed. "I know it's crazy." She

closed the book cover and leaned back on the stool.

"It's not crazy. It's important to you."

Mary gave her a weak smile. "I just feel like there must be something in these books. There has to be something I'm not seeing. I just wish there were someone I could ask."

"Have you talked to Sally Parks?"

"Who?"

Rebecca held out the book she'd been paging through and pointed to the acknowledgments page. Mary pulled the book closer.

The author of the book — a mystery with the house in the background — thanked her husband, her children, her agent, her editor, and "the incomparable Mrs. Sally Parks, assistant to the publisher, without whom this book would never have made it to press."

"You're a genius," Mary said.

"Keep reading."

"She knows everyone and everything at Hartell; without her, Hartell would surely cease to exist," Mary read out loud. "Thank you for all that you did." She scanned the rest of the page but didn't see the name Jacob thanked.

The thanks for Sally Parks was grand hyperbole, but still . . .

"She seems like she might be the kind of person who would know something about Jacob," Rebecca said.

"Why is it that things like this always seem so obvious once someone points them out?" Mary said. She'd never even thought to look at the acknowledgments page. Many books gave the author space to thank the people who contributed to the book in some way, but Mary usually skipped over them. Unless you knew the people thanked, they were little more than lists of names. But of course, it was an obvious place to learn the names of the people who the author felt contributed to the book. And this Sally Parks seemed like a good place to start.

Mary turned back to her computer and Googled the name Sally Parks. The first few hits that came up were Facebook pages for women several years younger than the Sally they were looking for. Mary looked down the page of search results. There was a park in Denver named after a man whose last name was Sally, and a family tree that turned up sisters named Sally and Selma Parks who had lived in the late nineteenth century. She clicked through several pages of search results, but nothing looked right.

"Go back to the first one," Rebecca suggested. "The first result is the closest match.

There's gotta be something there."

Mary thought it was a waste of time. This was clearly not the Sally they were looking for. But she didn't know what else to do, so she clicked back on the first link. It was the Facebook page of a girl at Tufts University named Sally Parks. Mary clicked around the page. The page didn't seem to have any restrictions, and Mary could see all her photos. If nothing else, it was good voyeurism. This Sally was on the university's field hockey team, which had apparently won its last game. She posted pictures of her lunch several days last week. There were birthday greetings from friends for her birthday several days ago. Mary idly clicked on her photos. There were pictures from a formal dance and from a friend's party. There were a few of Sally with the field hockey team. And there was an album from over a year ago labeled "Gram's 80th." Mary clicked on that.

The pictures showed Sally and what looked like a large extended family at an outdoor party. The food had been put out on elaborate iron outdoor furniture, and the house appeared to be large and grand. The family had gathered on the large lawn that sloped down to what looked like a boat dock. There were shots of Sally with her two brothers, with her cousins, and a large group shot of the whole clan, if the captions were to be believed. And, Mary noted, there was one of Sally sitting next to an elderly woman, her arm slung around her shoulders. The caption read: "Me and Gram, who I'm named after."

"What do you think the chances are that this is the Sally Parks we're looking for?" Mary asked, pointing at the woman in the photo. She was dressed in a brightly colored caftan and wore rings on every finger as well as several necklaces. She was laughing at the camera.

"I'd say pretty good," Rebecca said, leaning in closer. "She's the right age. And look." She gestured for Mary to go to the next picture in the album. Mary clicked on it and saw that it was a shot of both Sallys and what seemed like other family members standing outside an ice-cream shop in Centerville.

"Four Seas," Mary said. It was a famous shop in Centerville that sold some of the best ice cream on the Cape, aside from Bailey's, of course. Mary had been there many times. Which meant —

"She's local," Rebecca said.

Mary typed "Sally Parks Centerville" into an online white pages site and leaned back and smiled when a phone number popped up. Mary reached for the phone.

"She's going to think I'm nuts," she said.

"When has that ever stopped you before?" Rebecca said.

Mrs. Parks's phone rang several times, and as Mary listened to the rings, she tried to figure out what she'd say. She poised her finger over the End button in case she decided to disconnect the call, when someone finally answered.

"Hello there," a female voice answered.

"Oh, hello." She quietly cleared her throat. "My name is Mary Fisher. I'm looking for a Mrs. Parks."

"You've found me."

"Mrs. Parks, I know this will sound strange —"

"Call me Sally, honey. My husband's mother was Mrs. Parks, and I have to tell you, I didn't like her, not one little bit."

Mary bit her bottom lip to stop herself from laughing before she spoke again. "Okay, then. Sally. I know this will sound strange, but did you by any chance work at Hartell Press?"

"Oh yes," she said. "For several years. It was a wonderful place to work."

Mary heard a dog barking in the background. "I wondered if I could ask you some questions about some ol— well, some books I found."

Sally chuckled. "You can call them old. Most everyone I worked with is in the grave now."

Mary felt herself warming to this forthright woman. There was something refreshing about someone who said exactly what they thought. "Could I stop by your house tomorrow to ask you a few questions?"

"Why wait until tomorrow?"

"Well, I thought you might be busy."

"I'm never too busy for company, honey." She paused. "What did you say your name was?"

"Mary Fisher."

"Well, Mary, why don't you come my way this afternoon?"

Mary glanced at her watch. It was almost eleven now. "Really?"

"Of course. It's a lovely day for a drive."

Mary looked out the window of the back door, at the gray clouds that had taken over the blue sky. "I don't think —"

"Very good." Sally muttered something Mary didn't understand, and then she gave her elaborate directions along with her address.

"I'll expect you at four," Sally said before she hung up the phone.

152

Mary stared at the telephone in her hands. She didn't want to leave the shop for the afternoon, but she didn't want to delay this trip either. Sally could be the one to lead her to Jacob. At the very least, she might know his last name. Based on their short conversation, Mary suspected that if Sally had information to share, she would gladly disclose it.

"Do you mind watching the shop again this afternoon?" she asked.

"Of course not," Rebecca answered.

Mary tried not to get too excited, but she couldn't help it. She might be about to talk to the person who could lead her to Jacob.

TEN

Mary looked down at the directions Sally had given her. She lived a good fifteen minutes southeast of Centerville, on the Atlantic coast. It would be a nice drive. She checked her watch. It was too early to leave, but she hadn't been able to focus on anything else since she'd spoken with Sally.

Thanks to several hours of work by Betty and Rebecca, the shop was spotless and smelled like a harvest of autumn flowers. Ashley was now in the children's nook, after Russell had dropped her off after school because he'd had an errand to run, and she was pacing back and forth, looking down at her script. She'd been there since school let out, studying the script very studiously, and every once in a while, she'd let out a squawk that Mary guessed was supposed to sound like a duck.

When Mary got back from Sally's, it would be just about time to head over to the school for Ashley's performance. Mary was definitely looking forward to that. Then, she would return to the shop to finish inputting her receipts. Of course, if Sally could tell her anything about Jacob, her plans could change. She might spend much of her day — save for Ashley's play — tracking him down.

As Mary waited until it was time to go see Sally, she did a little research on the computer about the genetics of eye color. It seemed that it was possible for parents with brown eyes, like her father's, and green eyes, like her mother's, to have blue-eyed children, but it was rare. It would have been more likely if the father had blue or green eyes. Mary couldn't tell what color Jacob's eyes were in the black-and-white beach photo she'd tucked into her purse. She shook her head. This was getting her nowhere. She looked at her watch. It was still a few minutes before it was time to leave.

She decided to scan the letters with her color scanner, just so she would have copies of them in case. That took about ten minutes, but it still wasn't time to get going when she was done.

It was odd that Karly hadn't come in to the shop yet. Mary wondered if Jayne had given her the message that she'd wanted to

155

speak with her. She'd pop her head into Gems and Antiques before she left to see if she could catch her. She also checked her cell phone to see if Dawn had returned her call, but she hadn't. Strange.

Mary packed the books into her canvas bag and slung it over her shoulder, and patted her purse to make sure the letters and bracelet were where she'd put them. Gus was curled up by the radiator. "I should be back by five thirty," Mary told Rebecca. "Maybe a little earlier."

"Sounds good." Rebecca tapped her hand on the counter. "We have to leave for the school around then. We'll lock up if you're not back."

"Well, in case I don't see you before then," Mary said, walking over to where Ashley was pacing, "break a leg."

Ashley looked up from her script with a questioning look.

"That means good luck," Rebecca said. Ashley nodded and smiled, and Mary leaned in and gave her a hug.

"I'll be there cheering for you," Mary said, then headed toward the door.

"I'll just be glad when it's over," Rebecca said quietly as she came near. "She refused to eat a bite of breakfast this morning. She said she wasn't afraid, but her stomach was scared."

"I understand," Mary replied. If she was honest, she was a bit nervous about what she might discover today as well. She hoped Jacob was still alive, hoped that he might be able to share a bit of her mother's story with her. If she couldn't find out who delivered the books, she hoped that Sally could point her toward Jacob.

Before she went to her car, she walked across the street to Gems and Antiques.

"Back again?" Jayne said as she stepped inside. "Did Karly make it over to your store?"

"No, she never came by, so I thought I'd see if she was free now."

"I'm sorry, Mary, but Karly went home about an hour ago, when her shift ended. I told her you wanted to see her, so I thought she was coming to talk to you."

"That's strange," Mary said. Karly had seen that Mary wanted to talk with her earlier. So why hadn't she come by the shop, especially if she wanted those books? Mary shook her head. It didn't make sense. What was Karly hiding?

"Thanks, anyway," she said, and gave Jayne a wave as she ducked out of the shop. She zipped up her fleece jacket and hurried down the lane to her car.

The drive was beautiful. The sun peeked out through the clouds, and autumn leaves glittered in still ponds and lakes like her mother's jewelry had in the light. As much as she missed the friends she'd left behind in Boston, there was no place else that she'd rather be than right here on Cape Cod.

She turned off the highway and drove another two miles until she reached a lane along the Atlantic coast that was lined with huge homes. Mary drove a little slower as she searched for house numbers on the brick columns and gates that guarded many of the homes. They were spectacular. Sally Parks had done well for herself.

The gate to Sally Parks's palatial home was wide open. Mary steered her Impala up the paved lane to the sprawling mansion with crisp-white siding and pale-blue shutters. On the front lawn was a fountain with a grand swan in the center that reminded her of a fountain one might find in Paris or Milan. She'd never seen anything quite like it on Cape Cod. It didn't have the refined, understated elegance of many of the costly homes on the Cape, but she supposed it was nice in a different way.

Before she got out of the car, Mary checked her phone one more time to see if Dawn had called her back yet, but there were still no messages. If she hadn't heard from the woman by the time she returned to Ivy Bay, she would call her again. Tabitha had to know something about Jacob.

Mary walked toward Sally's house, pulling her jacket tighter around her. A face peeked out at her through the oval window beside the front door, and a dog yapped. Then the door swung open.

Sally Parks was a petite woman with muddy-blonde hair pulled back tight in a dark green bow. She wore an embroidered silk house robe and bunny slippers. In one arm was a dark brown teacup Chihuahua.

She held out her hands. "Welcome to my humble abode."

Mary cleared her throat. "Thank you. It's beautiful."

Sally leaned forward and kissed Mary on both cheeks. "Come in, come in, before you freeze to death." She punctuated her words with a little shiver and a quick rub of one arm. "This is Cocoa." She gestured at the dog.

The inside of the house reminded Mary of the floats she'd seen in Ivy Bay's Fourth of July parade — colorful and flashy. A

159

grand staircase rose to the second floor of the tiled entry, and an exotic chandelier dangled from the ceiling with colorful spirals of what looked like glass stars shooting out in all directions. Abstract pieces of artwork hung on the walls, painted with bright red, purple, and turquoise.

Sally motioned them toward the next room. "All the houses around here look just the same. I kept telling my Alfred, God rest his soul, that we needed something with a bit more flair, but he said this place was flair enough."

Mary studied the unusual shapes and colors on the artwork in front of her. She thought she would have to agree with Alfred. She followed Sally under an archway, into a living room packed with more things than Mary's bookshop. There were prints of animals on the walls, Oriental rugs on the floor, the stuffed head of a lion above a stone fireplace, small trees emerging from brightly colored planters, and an eclectic mixture of couches and chairs scattered randomly across the room. Windows lined the far wall of the room, and Mary moved toward them, watching the waves crash across the beach below them.

Mary brushed her hands over a light tan-and-black-striped couch that looked like it had been upholstered with some sort of animal skin. "This is unusual." She watched Sally with admiration. Instead of losing her zeal as the years crept past, she had obviously embraced her zest for life. She must keep her family quite entertained.

"It's from a zebra," Sally explained. "My husband used to hunt all over the world."

"He must have been an adventurous man."

Sally pointed up at the lion's head. "He shot that cat over in Namibia two months before he waved good-bye to this world."

"Did you meet your husband in New York?" Mary asked.

"I sure did. He was quite the rich businessman. He swept me off my feet."

Mary smiled indulgently. "When did you marry?"

"Back in '58." She sat down in a chair, set Cocoa on her lap, and crossed her bunny slippers. There was a bright orange teapot in the center of the coffee table. "I was an old maid by then, at the grand age of twenty-eight, but I was in no rush to get married. But then I met Alfred at a splendid little party in Manhattan. He was forty-nine and was in quite a rush to get me to the altar."

Mary tried to choose her words carefully.

"You must have been very much in love."

"I had quite a good life with Alfred, an amazing one, really, but looking back, I probably never should have left my job. I missed the work and my fabulous boss. You never know how good you have it until it's gone . . ." Her voice trailed off, and then she looked up at Mary. "If I got married today, I would have just kept on working at Hartell."

Mary reached for her bag. "Speaking of Hartell —"

"Ah yes. That's why you're here!" Sally leaned forward and poured her a cup of tea. "Please tell me you take real sugar in your tea?"

Mary nodded. "A little."

"Six years with that company — six wonderful years. We were small but quite reputable as a publishing house."

Mary took out three of the books and placed them on the mirrored coffee table encased by gold leaf. "Do you happen to remember these books? I think they were published by Hartell."

Sally reached out, her red nails brushing the top book as she took it in her hands. The sight of the books actually made her pause. "I haven't seen these for so many years, probably since I worked at the company."

"So you do remember them?"

"Of course I do. I remember all the books I worked on."

"We're particularly interested in learning more about the artist who did the cover art," Mary said, lifting up the next book in the stack. "The paintings are so beautiful, and it seems the same artist did them all."

"The artist?" Sally tilted her head, studying Mary for a moment. "What do you want to know about Stuart?" She dumped a generous portion of sugar in her cup and stirred it. "I haven't thought about him in a very long time."

Mary leaned toward her. "The artist's name was Stuart?"

Sally nodded. "Stuart Hendricks."

Mary swallowed her sigh. It had been a long shot, she supposed. All she had was one drawing on a letter, and she'd assumed . . .

Still, she had been so sure. She stared into her tea.

But somehow one of Stuart's drawings had ended up on Mom's letter. There had to be a connection of some sort.

Sally set down her teacup. "Stuart did the best covers in the entire publishing industry . . . or at least we at Hartell liked to think he did. My boss prided himself on being able to use Stuart's work whenever possible."

Mary took a sip of her tea. It was a very sweet Earl Grey. She put her tea bag on her saucer and added a bit of milk. "So you knew Stuart well?"

Sally sighed. "I never met him, but it wasn't for lack of trying. Stuart was a great artist, but he never made it into the office. He lived somewhere out here on the Cape. All his correspondence was by mail."

Mary leaned forward. "How many book covers did he create for you?"

"A few dozen or so. He did eight or so books right in a row for us, including these three, and then a bunch of layout and design for other covers."

Mary looked back toward the windows. It seemed an odd coincidence that he lived on the Cape if he wasn't somehow connected to all this. Maybe he knew Jacob?

"Do you know where Stuart is now?" Mary asked.

Sally laughed. "Probably dead. That was a long time ago, you know." She must have seen the surprise on Mary's face because she softened. "I'm sorry, dear. I have to laugh about it. Otherwise it just makes me sad. But no, I don't know what happened to Stuart. I lost touch with the people at Hartell when I stopped working there."

Sally talked about the apartment she'd had when she first moved to New York and about what it was like to work in publishing in the 1950s. Mary was only half listening, trying to work through what she knew, but it just didn't make sense. She'd reached a dead end.

Mary finished her tea. "Thank you so much for your time. I really appreciate your help, and I hate to leave so soon, but I've got a seat reserved for me at a children's performance of *Click, Clack, Moo*."

Sally clapped her hands. "Oh, I simply love the theater on any level."

Mary smiled. She was beginning to wonder if there was anything this woman didn't love.

"I used to go to Broadway at least once a month when I lived in New York. There was no place I'd rather be."

Mary stood up. The woman continued talking as Mary gathered her books and put her jacket back on. Sally held open the door and kissed both of Mary's cheeks. "Come back and visit me anytime."

A ray of light pushed its way through the clouds as Mary drove back toward Ivy Bay.

She didn't know any more about Jacob, but she had to smile anyway. She'd never met anyone quite like Sally before. And Mary would keep looking. She'd see what she could learn about this Stuart Hendricks. The drawing of the lighthouse on Mom's letter made her think Stuart was connected to Jacob or Mom somehow. If he was still alive and if she could track him down, he might have some answers.

She slowed at a stop sign, looked both ways, and kept driving.

Mary thought through what she knew and what she needed to find out.

If she could figure out who had left the box, she might find some answers. Maybe the cupcake sticker she'd found could point her in the right direction. She'd look into that more. She also needed to learn the connection between Jacob's letters and Stuart's drawings. She would still try to get a hold of Tabitha, and also try to figure out why Karly had wanted those books.

She didn't have a lot to go on. Mary started to wonder if she'd ever find the truth about Jacob.

ELEVEN

Mary stopped at a light in the historic downtown of Barnstable on the way back home. The town was bigger than Ivy Bay, but just as quaint, with its weathered houses and brick shops. She drove slowly up the main street of the town. A few people milled on the sidewalk, but the skies were spitting again; most people were headed for shops or restaurants to find shelter.

Mary wondered how she was going to find Stuart. The thought of calling everyone with the last name of Hendricks on Cape Cod sounded a bit daunting to her, but if that's what she had to do to find out more about Jacob, she would.

She glanced into the window of a pet shop and saw two cats climbing up a stand. Next to it was a pizza shop, and in the next window was a —

She stared at the sign above the shop. The car behind her honked, and Mary drove forward, but pulled over to side of the road and parked at the curb in front of the shop. She looked up at the logo of a pink, yellow, and mint-green cupcake on the sign. She'd seen that logo before. She dug in her purse for the sticker with the cupcake on it.

The cupcake on the sticker was yellow and pink against a mint background, just like on the sign. Under the cupcake, in fancy script, it read: Karen's Cupcakes. A neat hand-lettered sign in the window said Coming Soon.

Could this have been where the books had come from? But this was a good fifteen-minute drive from her bookshop. Mary knew there were other bookstores closer than her shop. So why had someone driven to Ivy Bay? Mary grabbed her umbrella from behind the seat and unlocked her door.

If she hurried, she could investigate this and still make it back in time for Ashley's play.

The front door of the cupcake shop was locked, and she didn't see anyone inside, though there was a glass display case against the wall and several tall stacks of boxes. Two walls were painted the same mint and pink from the sticker, and the far wall was white. There were white shelves inlaid in the wall to her right, behind the display cases. She could imagine them filled with all sorts of decorated boxes and sweet treats. It didn't look like it would be long before Karen's Cupcakes opened.

Mary hurried back to her car and wrote a short note on the back of an envelope, asking Karen to call her. She scribbled her phone number and slid the envelope into the mail slot on the front door. If Karen didn't call her, she'd make another trip back to Barnstable tomorrow.

Mary was only ten minutes late to Liberty Elementary School that evening and wouldn't have even been late at all except she wanted to stop by Tanaka Florist and Garden Center and buy a red rose for her favorite actress.

Ashley shone on the stage in her role as the duck. She wore a white leotard and tights and a hat with a duck bill on it, and she carried an old-fashioned typewriter between the cows and the farmer, and was such a ham that Mary suspected she might have a future in theater ahead of her. Seeing Ashley up there made Mary miss her grandchildren. Emma was so quiet and serious, but had a wicked sense of humor, and her brother Luke was a tornado of energy. And teenage Daisy was in that stage of testing out her independence, but she still enjoyed being around her parents. They were each so special and precious, and Mary thanked God for them.

When the show finished, the audience stood to applaud the performers. The children bowed over and over, smiling with delight in the blue canned lights. After the curtain was drawn, Mary greeted Ashley with a long hug. "You are like the Shirley Temple of the stage!"

Ashley tilted her head. "Who's Shirley Temple?"

"A cute little actress just like you," Mary said with a laugh as she slipped the flower out from behind her back. "Every good performer deserves a rose."

Ashley eyed the rose warily. "Are there thorns?"

"Not a single one."

Ashley clutched the rose to her chest, and she was quickly surrounded by children admiring her gift. Mary couldn't have been more proud of the girl, for her hard work and determination. She lingered for ten more minutes, enjoying the celebration. Then she popped her umbrella over her head, and she hurried back in the drizzle to the bookshop. She still hadn't gotten those invoices done, and she needed to get that finished.

Rebecca forgot to turn the front sign to Shut when she had left the shop that afternoon, so Mary flipped the sign as she stepped inside. The desk lamp lit the countertop, but all the other lights were off, so Mary turned them on. She sat down on the tall stool and logged into the computer. As she waited for her computer to boot up, she reached for her cell phone. It was so strange that Dawn hadn't called her back today to set up a time for Mary and Tabitha to get together. Could she have forgotten? It was only eight o'clock. Tabitha might have gone to bed, but even if she had, Dawn would probably still be awake. She dialed Tabitha's home number, and it rang several times, but no one picked up. Eventually, Mary hung up. Mary stared down at the screen of her phone for a moment. In the past, Tabitha had been excited about spending time with Mary, and Dawn had always been responsive. Was Mary just being paranoid, or was Tabitha really avoiding her now?

She took the sticker out of her purse and typed Karen's Cupcakes into her Internet browser. The search brought up dozens of cupcake shops with the same name, so she added Barnstable to her search, but with this criteria, she didn't get a single result.

She leaned back against the stool, looking at the screen. Karen's Cupcakes hadn't even opened yet; she couldn't expect that she would find it with a basic Internet search. She clicked her mouse again until she found the Cape Cod Chamber of Commerce site, scrolling through the names of businesses until she found Karen's Cupcakes. There was no contact information, but the name Karen Rivers was listed as the business owner.

Mary stared at the woman's last name. Was it possible that Karen was related to Max Rivers, the owner of the Rivers Accounting firm here in Ivy Bay? Mary did her own accounting, so she had never used the firm's services. But hadn't Lori Stone told her that the Rivers Accounting Firm was closing? Could that somehow be connected to the Karen she was looking for?

Someone knocked on the door, and Mary jumped, her head turning toward the front of the store. It wasn't *too* late, not like it had been on Monday night, but it was still strange to have someone stop by after dark. Mary held her breath for a moment, not sure what to expect, until Karly Sundin's face appeared in the glass panes on the door. Mary released her breath.

Mary scrambled around the counter to

unlock the door. "Well, hi there, Karly."

She wore the same striped scarf around her neck and a cherry-red wool hat.

Karly pointed back at the sign. "I know you're closed, but when I saw you in here, I thought I would pop in. I'm sorry I didn't come by earlier. I had to drive my grandfather to a doctor's appointment and had to get home as soon as my shift was over. But I wanted to come by since Jayne said I would."

Mary let out her breath. Here she'd assumed Karly had been hiding something when she didn't come by this afternoon, and she had actually been taking care of her grandfather. And she had followed through on a commitment someone else had made on her behalf. Maybe Mary had misjudged her. But still, Karly *had* recognized the books, and then she'd tried to buy them. She did know something more than she was telling.

"I'm glad you came by." Mary pointed toward the chairs in the back near the fireplace. "Do you want to have a seat?"

Karly unwrapped her scarf and dropped her handbag beside one of the chairs. "For just a minute. I don't want to keep you."

"It's no trouble at all. I was hoping we could reconnect. It was so nice to chat with you yesterday." Mary meant what she said, but she also wanted to know more about why Karly had acted so strangely.

Mary turned on the fireplace and scooted the bouquet of flowers a few inches back on the table so she could see Karly's face. "Jayne said you're a great saleswoman."

"I'm so glad, because I've been really enjoying the work," Karly said as she crossed her legs. "And I'll have Sundays and Mondays off to go take pictures."

"It's great that you'll still be able to do something you care about."

The heater kicked on, and a low hum filled the quiet store.

Mary straightened the hem of her sweater. "Karly, I wanted to ask you about those books I showed you the other day. The ones with the coastal pictures on the covers. You seemed to recognize them. Have you seen them before the other day?"

Karly hesitated for a moment and then shook her head. "I think they must have just reminded me of something else." Her black boot pumped up and down.

"Rebecca told me you came in and tried to buy them."

Karly opened her mouth and then closed it again. Then, slowly, she nodded. "I thought that cover you showed me was so beautiful," she said. "As an artist, I really appreciated them, and I wanted to study them more carefully."

Karly's boot pumped a little faster. Her story was plausible enough, but she seemed nervous.

"It is nice artwork, isn't it?"

Karly nodded. "I'd still love to buy those books if you're willing to part with them. I was hoping that's what you'd asked me here for."

Mary leaned back in her chair. "I'm afraid they're not for sale, at least not right now. I'm trying to find out who delivered them to me." Mary took a deep breath. "You wouldn't happen to know who brought me these books, would you?"

Karly shook her head. "I have no idea." She tapped her fingers on her leg. "But maybe there's something inside the books that will tell you. Did you —" She paused and then cleared her throat. "Did you look through the books carefully?"

Mary watched the girl. Did she know about the letters? Was that what she had wanted when she offered to buy the books?

"There's nothing inside the books that points me to my benefactor," she said, carefully sidestepping Karly's question.

Mary didn't think Karly had delivered the

175

books, especially after seeing Karen's Cupcakes and the matching logo from the sticker. Plus, why would she have dropped the books off if she wanted them so badly? But she wasn't quite certain that the young woman didn't know who'd owned these books. Was she trying to buy them back for someone?

Mary tapped her fingers on the arm of the chair. Part of her wanted to be honest with this girl about the letters in the books, if only to see her reaction, but she needed to be cautious with this information until she found out more about Jacob. For now, the secret would stay with her, Betty, Rebecca, and, of course, Henry, but he was practically family. He wouldn't share her secret.

Karly stood up. "Well, I should probably get going."

Mary stood up beside her. "Of course."

"If you decide to sell those books," Karly said as she wrapped her scarf around her neck, "I'd like to buy all eight of them."

"I'll remember," Mary assured her. It would be awfully hard to forget the woman's interest in them.

Mary watched Karly walk down the street and climb into a vintage blue Volkswagen Bug. Where had she come from, and what did she know about the owner of these books?

Mary sat back down in front of her computer, but she couldn't focus on the invoices. Her mind kept wandering back to the letters, the book covers, the mysterious sketch, Jacob . . . and Betty. Betty didn't seem willing to believe what the letters suggested, but Mary would find out the truth so they could both deal with it, whatever it was.

Mary gave up and slowly turned out the lights in the shop. She would go home tonight and finish reading *The Cellar Door* and maybe even have a dish of pumpkin ice cream.

As she locked the door and started home, she stared over at the dark window of Gems and Antiques. Mary thought back to her first meeting with Karly, and she realized something. She'd never told Karly how many books there were; she had only shown her the top two from the box. How had she known there were eight of them?

TWELVE

After dinner, Mary's daughter Lizzie called to say hi, and Mary got a chance to talk to her grandchildren Luke and Emma. It did her heart good to hear them talk about their lives, and it was a little after ten when Mary finished her bowl of pumpkin ice cream and read another chapter of her novel. She climbed into bed, but her mind continued to race as she mulled over all that happened during the day, plowing through question after question. She had thought Jacob was the artist for the book covers, but according to Sally, he wasn't. It was Stuart Hendricks. If Stuart was the designer, Mary was nearly convinced that he must have been the one who'd drawn the sketch on her mother's letter. But how had he had any access to her mother's books and the letters within, and did he know anything about Jacob?

There was also the question of Karly. What did Karly Sundin know about the books, and why was she so reluctant to tell Mary about it? And what was the connection between the books and Karen's Cupcakes in Barnstable? Her thoughts turned to Tabitha. Dawn had never gotten back to her today. Could it have been possible that Tabitha was hiding something too?

Moonlight streamed into Mary's bedroom window as she adjusted her pillow before she slept. Not only did she have the books on her mind, but *Cape Cod Living* was coming the day after tomorrow. She had to begin thinking again about her preparations. The shop was clean, but she hadn't even begun to think about what she would wear. She sighed, adjusting her pillow again. She wouldn't be able to answer any of her questions about the books or prepare for Friday's interview if she didn't get some sleep.

She closed her eyes and began to quietly quote one of her favorite Bible verses. "I will lie down and sleep in peace, for you alone, O Lord, make me dwell in safety."

She wasn't in danger, but she needed her mind to dwell in and on Him tonight so she could sleep peacefully instead of thinking through all her unanswered questions. Tomorrow, she would go back to Tabitha's house in the morning and ask her in person if she knew Jacob. She would try to find information about Stuart Hendricks. And if she had to, she would drive back to Barnstable to find Karen Rivers and ask her if she was the one who dropped the books off at her shop. Mary snuggled into her pillow and tried to relax, but it was a long time before she finally fell asleep.

Mary woke up early the next morning, and she got out of bed at first light. But before she showered, she picked out a soft cable-knit cashmere sweater, a gift from Betty, that she'd thought about as she finally fell asleep last night. It was an attractive navy blue, and she thought it would look nice for the photo shoot tomorrow, but she wanted to take another look to make sure it was ready. As she lifted the dry cleaner's plastic cover, she gasped. There was a hole in the sleeve, right along the seam. She couldn't have a photographer take her picture with a hole in her sleeve. She didn't remember ripping it, but at this point, it didn't matter how the damage happened. She'd have to get it repaired. She would have to find a tailor and hope they would have mercy on her and mend it for her today. If not, she'd have to fix it up herself with safety pins for the morning.

After Mary dressed in a cherry-red turtleneck and a matching black-and-red sweater, she slipped down the hallway and carpeted stairs. Betty was still in her room, so Mary moved quietly into the kitchen and started the coffeemaker. Then she slathered a piece of wheat toast with peach jam. She loved the quiet of the early morning hours as the peace of God settled over the entire town. Below the window, Betty's garden was blanketed with mist. Hundreds of birds fluttered in the trees, probably preparing to head south for the winter, their feathers swallowed up in the fog. Mary was anxious to take the sweater to a tailor's to be repaired, and she hoped to pop over to the county records room to see if she could find any information about Jacob or Stuart Hendricks, but neither of those places would be open yet. But there was one place she could go this early. She finished her coffee, set the cup in the dishwasher, and then pulled on a thick wool coat. Before she left the house, Mary promised Gus that she would return for him and the torn sweater before she opened the shop.

The sun was beginning to chase away the fog as Mary got into her car and drove toward Tabitha's home. It was a little after eight as Mary stepped up to the door. Mary knew her friend was an early riser, and she hoped she could catch her and ask her about the books and about Jacob. She hoped Tabitha wouldn't think she was being rude showing up so early, but in the past, Tabitha had made it clear that Mary and Betty were always welcome at her house. She hit the iron knocker again and waited as the minutes slipped by, hoping Dawn would open the door like she had on Tuesday. This time, though, no one responded to her knock.

Mary waited another minute and then rang the doorbell. She could hear its echo through the door, but still no one answered it. After another minute of waiting, she stepped off the porch and looked up at the windows and tower, hoping to catch some sort of light or movement, but all seemed still in Tabitha Krause's home. Had Tabitha gone somewhere early this morning? Or was Tabitha hiding from her?

As Mary walked back to her car, she realized how crazy that sounded. Tabitha had been her mother's best friend. Why would she be hiding from Mary? But it did seem strange that the one person who would be able to answer Mary's questions was suddenly unavailable to her. Was it possible she knew the truth about Betty and didn't want Mary to find out? Mary hoped the elderly woman was okay. Maybe she would call Tabitha's granddaughter Amelia later and make sure she wasn't ill.

Mary drove back through town toward her house, but she took an indirect route that led her down Liberty Road, where the Rivers Accounting firm was based. Lori had said the business was closing, but perhaps they were still cleaning out the office and getting things finished. It was at least worth driving by to see if she could track down Karen, if indeed the Karen Rivers she wanted to talk with was related to Max Rivers.

There weren't many businesses on this street, which was largely taken up by the athletic fields of Liberty Elementary School, but there was a cluster of small storefronts housed in a row of brick townhouses at the corner of Meeting House Road. Mary slowed as she drove past, and she saw the words *Rivers Accounting* painted on the plate-glass window of one of the storefronts. There was a small For Sale sign in the corner. The lights were on. Mary parked the car and hopped out, and then she headed to the storefront. Mary peeked in the window and saw a plump woman was already working inside, wearing a Boston Red Sox cap and an oversized gray sweatshirt. The woman's back was to the glass door, so Mary knocked gently, not wanting to startle her. The woman turned quickly, and when she saw Mary, she crossed the room and opened the door to greet Mary with a polite smile.

"I'm sorry," she said as she opened the door. She glanced back at the pile of boxes behind her. "We're closing our office."

Mary nodded. "I heard. It must be hard to say good-bye to your family's business."

"Part of me is sad, I suppose, but accounting was my husband's passion." She ducked her head. "He passed away last month."

"Oh." Mary had known that the business was closing, but she hadn't known why. That was terrible news. "I'm so sorry to hear that," Mary said, and she felt a familiar ache in her stomach. She hadn't known Max well, but she'd met him a few times, and it was always sad to hear of someone's passing. But even more, she felt her heart wrench for this woman. It wasn't so long ago that Mary had been left a widow, and Mary knew the overriding feeling of hopelessness and sadness Max's wife must be feeling right now. That was enough to deal with, and just making it through the day had felt like a struggle in the first few months, but having to deal with practical matters, like cleaning out John's things, on top of that, had been nearly overwhelming. She knew that it couldn't be easy for this lady to be sorting through the remains of her husband's business now. "I lost my husband a while back, and I know how hard it can be." She gave the woman an encouraging smile, though her heart ached.

"Thank you." The woman pulled the door open a bit wider. "I'm trying to get it all cleaned out as quickly as possible, but it's taking longer than I thought, since every file seems to bring back memories. It's amazing all you can collect in thirty years."

Mary nodded. She knew that feeling. "I know I wanted to just get my husband's things all sorted out, but then when it was all done, I wasn't sure what to do with myself."

"I'm trying to keep busy." The woman pushed back the brim of her hat. "So what can I do for you?"

"I'm looking for Karen Rivers," Mary said, eyeing her to gauge her reaction.

"That's me," Karen said.

"Are you by any chance opening up a bakery in Barnstable?"

The woman nodded slowly, obviously confused.

"I drove past your new shop yesterday. It

looks adorable," Mary said. "My name is Mary Fisher." She stretched out her hand, and Karen shook it.

"Oh, you left a note. I haven't had a chance to call you yet, but I was planning to," Karen said. She pulled the door open a bit wider. "Would you like to come in?"

"Thank you," Mary said as she stepped inside. "This is a nice space." Every surface was piled with boxes, but the walls were painted a soothing sea green, and the floor was made of wide-plank pine. The office furniture was elegant dark wood, and there were framed pictures and knickknacks to soften up the office. It felt homey and welcoming — not at all what Mary would have expected an accountant's office to be like.

"Thanks," Karen said, looking around the small office. "We wanted people to feel comfortable here. Most people don't enjoy having conversations about the finances or having their taxes done, and we tried to make it as painless as possible."

"You didn't want to use this for your bakery?" Mary trailed her fingers along the smooth surface of the reception desk.

"Oh no," Karen said, laughing softly. "I didn't want to compete with Sweet Susan's. She makes the best cupcakes around, and everybody knows it. Plus, I'm moving to Barnstable. That's where my family is, and I'd like to be closer to them now." Karen moved a stack of file folders and gestured for Mary to sit on one of the reception chairs.

"I understand that." Mary lowered herself into the soft leather chair. "I moved here to open up a bookshop when my husband passed away."

"Oh, so you're the Mary who owns Mary's Mystery Bookshop?"

Mary nodded. "In fact, that's actually what I wanted to talk to you about. Someone dropped off a box of books outside my store the other night. I was wondering if you knew anything about them." She watched Karen, waiting to see if she flinched and reacted strangely. But instead, Karen seemed to come to life.

"Oh, good, so you found them. I was hoping they hadn't gotten damaged by the rain."

"So . . ." Mary tried to make her mouth form coherent words. "So *you* dropped them off?"

"Yes." Karen tilted her head. "Was that all right?"

Mary nodded, pressing her lips together for a moment. Finally, she had an answer to one of her many questions. This woman before her had dropped the books off on her doorstep. But that knowledge only raised a hundred new questions in her mind.

THIRTEEN

"Why did you just leave the books, with no note or anything?" Mary had a hundred questions to ask Karen about the books she'd left, but for some reason, it was the practical questions that came out first.

"Oh no," Karen said, tugging on the bottom of her sweatshirt. "Didn't I leave a note?"

Mary shook her head.

"I'm so sorry. I've been pretty scattered lately, to put it mildly. If I didn't have my head screwed on —" She paused.

Mary had to laugh at how frightened she'd been that night, when in the end, it had only been Karen outside her shop. But how did Karen Rivers, a woman she'd never met, come into possession of the same books that her mother once owned?

"How did you happen to have the books?"

Karen waved her hand. "I found them when I was cleaning out the basement here, and I didn't want to just throw them away. But I've been so frantic trying to get this place cleaned out and the bakery opened that it was late by the time I was ready to go. I figured it was easiest to just drop them where you'd find them."

"So you didn't . . ." Mary tried to figure out how to phrase this. "There was nothing special about the books?"

Karen shook her head. "It seemed a shame to get rid of them. I just wanted them to find a good home." The woman gave her a quizzical look. "Is something wrong with the books?"

"Well, not exactly wrong —" Mary formulated her words carefully. "Are the books yours?"

Karen shook her head and pointed at a door toward the back of the building. "I found them in the cellar with a whole bunch of old art supplies and a box of random stuff, so they must have belonged to a previous tenant. I took the books to you and put everything else in the trash."

Art supplies? Mary caught her breath. "Do you have any idea who owned the art supplies?"

Karen shrugged. "I heard that someone owned an art studio here before us, but I don't know the artist's name. We've been here thirty years, so even if I heard the name once, it's long gone."

"You don't still have that trash by any chance, do you?" Mary asked. Trash pickup only happened on Fridays, so there was a chance it hadn't been carted off to the dump yet.

Karen gave her a strange look, and Mary realized that it probably did seem like a bizarre request. She laughed. "I promise I don't normally go digging through people's garbage," she said, and Karen gave her a smile. "It's just that if an artist had a studio here, I'd be very interested in seeing what he left behind."

"That's okay." Karen nodded. "It's all still out in the back. Would you like me to get it for you?"

Mary knew it was a long shot. And rooting through somebody's trash to find answers was not exactly high on her list of fun things to do. But if there was any chance that stuff could lead her to answers about Jacob, she was willing to give it a shot.

"If you don't mind, I would appreciate it," Mary said.

"I'll be right back." Karen turned and disappeared out a door at the back of the office. Rain began to fall outside, and Mary glanced behind her. It soaked the front

191

window of the shop. What was the connection between Jacob, Stuart Hendricks, and this art studio?

"Here you go," Karen said, returning a few minutes later. "They're a little wet, but this is everything I found." She put a dusty cardboard box and a plastic bag full of tubes of paint on the desk. Mary could see that the box was filled with a jumble of receipts, envelopes, and newspaper clippings. "I wish I had more information for you," Karen said. "Was there something special about the books that I hadn't realized?"

Mary weighed her words carefully. "I found some letters inside of those books, written by my mother."

"Are you kidding?" Karen chuckled. "What are the chances?"

"I'm hoping the person who owned the books can tell me a little more about them," Mary said.

"Well, I hope you find some answers in that stuff," Karen said. "And please let me know if there's anything more I can do. I'll be here cleaning this place out," Karen said, gesturing around the office. There was still a fair amount to do, but even once this was done, Mary knew she could find her at the bakery in Barnstable.

"Thank you," Mary said, knowing she

meant it. One thing she'd learned since John died was that other widows were often willing to go far out of their way to help someone who had also lost a husband. She silently thanked God for this small blessing, even though it came out of tragedy.

Mary thanked Karen again and tucked the box and bag under her arm and stepped back onto the sidewalk. She had hoped Karen Rivers would answer her questions, but speaking with her only raised even more. How had her mother's books ended up at Rivers Accounting? Was it possible that the art studio had anything to do with Stuart Hendricks, and if so, why did Stuart have her mother's books and the letters she had written? And more important, what did he have to do with her mother and Jacob?

Mary stopped by the house to pick up the sweater and Gus. Betty was eating breakfast, and Mary asked her if she knew anything about an old art studio on Liberty Road, but she didn't remember it. Mary would try to look into it more today. Then she drove back and parked on Main Street and headed in to the shop. She put the box and bag on the counter, let Gus out of his carrier, and hung up her coat and stored her sweater in the back room. Then she brewed a pot of coffee at the beverage station before the shop opened. After Rebecca arrived, Mary planned to pay a visit to the county clerk's office, and she also wanted to get her sweater mended. But first, she wanted to dig through her new finds.

Hazy sunlight was filtering in through the front window, but heavy clouds were gathering. It looked like more rain was on the way. Gus was curled up in front of the radiator behind the counter. He had the right idea. It would be the perfect day to curl up in front of a fire with a good book. One of these days, Mary would have to keep the shop closed and just stay home and indulge in a reading day. She thought longingly of *The Cellar Door.* She was so close to finishing it. But today, she had too much she needed to get done.

She started with the plastic grocery bag of paints. There were a dozen or so tubes of oil paints, all made by a company called Tru-Blend, and a few tins of dried-out watercolors. There were many rich colors, from deep-russet reds to eggplant purple to spring green, but the majority of the paints were various shades of blue. Shades that would be useful if you want to paint scenes by the sea, Mary mused. She looked through all the paints carefully, but she didn't see anything that looked like a clue. She set the paints aside and opened the box. It was a mess of papers. She took out a handful from the top and set them in front of her. The first few pieces of paper were old bills addressed to Hendricks Studios, and then there were a handful of postcards announcing shows at art galleries. Mary pulled out another handful and found a write-up in the local paper of a show featuring the work of Stuart Hendricks.

Mary read the article quickly. The article talked about the paintings in the show, which were, according to the paper, seascapes. There was a photograph of one of the pieces in the show, and it showed a craggy cliff over a turbulent sea. It looked like it could have been on one of the book covers in Mary's box.

Mary sat back. So Sally had been right. Stuart was the artist who had done the book covers. And it seemed very likely that Stuart had owned the storefront on Liberty Road before the Rivers Accounting firm. But so far, she hadn't found anything that could tell her more about Stuart or how he was connected to Mom and Betty.

Mary pulled out more of the papers and sorted through them, but she didn't see anything that could give her answers. She was about to pile the old papers back in the box, but then she saw one more newspaper clipping caught by the flap of the cardboard box. She tugged it out gently.

It was a lengthy article, and Mary skimmed it quickly. It was an article about a theft that occurred during a Fourth of July celebration at the home of a prominent family named the Willards. Judging by the length of the story, either theft didn't occur very often in Ivy Bay during the 1940s or the Willards were quite an important family. According to the writer, tens of thousands of dollars in cash and other heirlooms were stolen from the family's vault in an upstairs den while hundreds of people were celebrating the holiday in both the Willards' house and on their two acres of landscaped property.

Mary read the article again, but it didn't yield any more information the second time through. Why did Stuart have this clipping? Could he have been connected to the theft somehow? Could it have been his family that had been robbed? Mary put the clipping down and rubbed her temples. It seemed likely that Stuart had his art studio here, and it seemed that his painting style matched the artwork on the book covers.

But that didn't get her any closer to finding Stuart.

The bell over the door chimed, and Rebecca walked in to the shop, carrying with her a rush of cold air and the smell of baking bread. Rebecca took off her wet jacket and shook it out. "Hello, there," she said. There were dark circles under her eyes.

"There's fresh coffee in the back." Mary laughed. "Did you stay up late with our little duck?"

"She was wound up, for sure, and the ice cream we got as a treat after the play didn't help much," Rebecca said. "I had to coax her into bed at ten. Of course, that made getting out of bed even more difficult this morning."

"The life of a celebrity is hard."

"The life of a celebrity's mother is even harder."

Mary laughed as Rebecca gave a long sigh, then walked toward the back. She hung up her coat and poured herself a cup of coffee, then came back to the front of the store. Mary was piling the papers back into the box.

"What do you have there?" Rebecca took a sip of coffee and sighed.

"A box full of nothing, as far as I can tell," Mary said, but her mind went back to the article she'd read. What did it have to do with anything? She lifted it off the counter and set it in one of the cubbies behind the counter. "It's from the same place the books came from." Mary filled her in on what she'd learned this morning, and Rebecca nodded appreciatively.

"So now you know that Stuart Hendricks was the artist of the book covers and that he rented that space out," Rebecca said. "What else do you know about him?"

"Not much," Mary said with a sigh.

"But I have a suspicion you're going to try to find out," Rebecca said, laughing.

"You know me too well." Mary looked at the clock. It was just past ten o'clock, so she got up and flipped the sign on the door over to Open. "I was hoping to run a few errands this morning. Would you mind watching the shop?" She eyed the stack of invoices still waiting to be entered. Well, they would still be there later.

"Of course not. Take your time."

A customer came into the shop, and Rebecca greeted her and directed her toward the shelf of cozies. Mary pulled the yellow pages off the shelf behind the counter and turned to the *T*'s. She ran her finger down the list of tailors. When she had stopped by the house earlier, Betty had recommended

Hamilton Tailors, where she always took her clothes to be mended, out on Route 6A. She found the listing and called the number to ask if they could take her sweater today. The woman who picked up was very nice, but told her she was working on dresses for a wedding party and there was no way she would be able to turn Mary's sweater around today. Mary thanked her and hung up, then ran her finger down the list of tailors in Ivy Bay: Press and Go Tailors, Olde Goode Clothiers, Sand Dollar Dry Cleaners . . . Her finger stopped on the next entry: Willards' Tailors.

It was too much a coincidence. There was no way it was the same Willards. The Willards in the article were wealthy, at least in the forties and these Willards owned a clothing-repair shop.

But still, she *did* need to find a tailor. Why not try this one? The worst that could happen was that she'd get her sweater repaired.

Mary wrote down the address and tucked it into her purse, along with the newspaper clipping she'd first read just a few minutes ago, grabbed her sweater from the back room, and then waved to Rebecca and headed out the door. She was grasping at straws, she knew, but straws were all she had at this point.

FOURTEEN

The rain started again before Mary parked her car beside the Willards' tailor shop, a small clapboard building with mauve shutters and a white picket fence around its yard. Behind the shop, on the same lot, was a white two-story home with matching shutters. Mary glanced at her dashboard clock and saw it was already ten thirty. She hoped they weren't busy today and could handle her small job, but either way, it was worth at least seeing if there was anything that connected the family that owned this shop to Stuart. She would head over to the county clerk's office as soon as she was done here, and hopefully she'd find more answers there.

With her sweater draped over her arm and covered by the wide umbrella, Mary pushed open the door to the shop. A brown-and-black hound dog rested on the floor just inside. The dog lifted his head ever so slightly, gave one bark like he was announcing her arrival, and then settled his head back on his paws again.

She laughed. "You and Gus would get along well," she said before she called out to the empty space, "Hello?"

She stepped into the next room of the old shop. The room was filled with racks of hanging clothes, three sewing machines, mirrors, and tabletops covered with pincushions and reels of thread.

"Is anyone here?" she called out again.

This time, she heard a woman's voice reply, "I'm back here."

Mary slid open a particle-board door and found an elderly woman sitting in a cushioned chair beside a minirefrigerator and sink. Her hair was hidden under a pink-and-yellow scarf, and her glasses were strung around her neck on a long silver chain. She wore a pink sweater and comfortable white slacks, and in front of her was a card table with several hundred puzzle pieces scattered across it.

"Don't just stand there." The woman motioned for Mary to join her. "I can't find the last two pieces for the clock."

Mary smiled and stepped closer to her, looking at all the pieces. So far, the woman had put together a bell tower leading up to

Big Ben, and most of the clock face. Mary set down her sweater and pushed around the remaining pieces, searching through the blue pieces of sky and brown pieces from the palace attached to the tower. Finally, she found the small hand of the clock.

"Here it is." Mary scooped it up and scooted it toward the woman.

"Bravo!" the woman said. "Only one more piece to go."

Mary searched the table again until she found it.

The woman eagerly finished the clock, and then she sat back and looked up at Mary, almost like she realized for the first time that she didn't know her. "How can I help you?"

Mary froze. The woman was wearing a necklace made of emeralds, with small diamonds on either side of the larger green stones. It was identical to the bracelet she'd found in the attic the other day.

Mary moved a folding chair toward the table and sat down next to her. "Well" — she tried to regain her composure — "I have a sweater that needs repair." She gestured to where it hung on the back of the door. "I was hoping to find someone who could stitch up the seam."

"I'm Ruthanne," the woman said simply.

"And you need Teresa."

"Teresa?" Mary asked, glancing back out the door like she might have missed someone.

"My daughter-in-law. She runs the store now." Her wrinkled hands shook as she reached for a piece and added it to the palace. "I can still do puzzles, but my fingers don't cooperate with a needle or thread anymore. Teresa is an excellent seamstress, though. Even better than I used to be."

Ruthanne leaned forward to reach for another puzzle piece, and her necklace dangled in front of her.

"Ruthanne, do you mind if I ask where you got that beautiful necklace?"

Ruthanne's fingers slipped to her throat and she tenderly fingered the piece. "It was from my family's collection. It was the only one left . . ." Her voice trailed off, and then she reached for another puzzle piece.

Mary leaned closer, her thoughts racing to catch up. "Left from . . . ?"

The clarity in the woman's eyes had started to fade when she looked at Mary again. "Who did you say you were?"

"I'm Mary Fisher. And my mother was Esther Randlett Nelson. Perhaps you knew her?"

Ruthanne nodded slightly, like she should

know the names but couldn't remember them. Mary quickly dug the photo of her mother on the beach out of her purse and slipped it across the table to the lady. "Do you recognize either this man or woman?"

Ruthanne pointed at Mary's mother. "She sure was a pretty girl."

"You didn't know her?"

"Sorry." Ruthanne shook her head. "I don't recognize her. But that's Jacob she's with."

Mary sat back, stunned. She couldn't believe that here, at the tailor shop of all places, she'd finally met someone who had known Jacob.

"So you know Jacob?"

"Oh yes," Ruthanne said. She leaned back against the chair, and her cheeks flushed. She seemed like she was about to say something, but then hesitated.

"How did you know him?" Mary prodded gently.

"He went to Barnstable High," Ruthanne said, shaking her head. "Our rivals. He was older than I was, but all the girls knew who he was. Of course, most of our young men were off at war, so the pickings were slim, but there was still something special about Jacob." Ruthanne reached for another puzzle piece, clicking it into place.

"This is my mother in the photograph." Mary pointed at her mother's face. "She passed away five years ago, and I just found this picture, and I'm hoping to find out more about the man with her."

"I see. Well, like I said, I didn't know your mother, although she looks lovely."

Mary sorted through the pieces in front of her and pulled out several that seemed to belong to a wall of the Tower of London.

"Do you know what happened to Jacob?"

Ruthanne leaned back in her chair, closing her eyes again. For a moment, Mary thought she had fallen asleep, but she lifted her head one more time, sighing before she spoke again. "Jacob was the quarterback of the Barnstable high school's football team." Ruthanne folded her hands on her lap. Her eyes opened, but they seemed to stare past Mary like she was watching her own memories on the wall. "I was a cheerleader, and I always secretly cheered for Jacob. I figured he would be a great success at whatever he put his mind to."

Ruthanne looked back down at the picture again on the table. "He was such a handsome boy. Tall and strong, and a bit wild, though he never seemed to be in trouble like some of my classmates."

"Do you know what happened to Jacob?"

Mary tried again.

It was like Ruthanne didn't even hear her. "During the summers, he fished alongside his father."

Mary decided to try a different tactic. "So he was close to his family?"

Ruthanne nodded. "He had a sister who was really sick. He was very close with her."

Mary leaned closer to the woman. "What was wrong with his sister?"

Ruthanne clicked her tongue. "Tuberculosis, I think."

Mary cringed. She knew that in the 1940s, tuberculosis could have been fatal.

"He and his family lived in a small cottage on the bay until Jacob joined the army. Then Patty and the rest of the family moved away to find her treatment."

"Did Jacob ever come back to Barnstable?"

"I don't know," she said with a slight shake of her head. "Many of the boys who were in the army left town after they came home. I suppose the town reminded them of something they wanted to forget. Jacob only joined after the war was over, but maybe he wanted to forget too. I never heard anything about Jacob again."

Mary took this in. Had he joined the army when he found out Mom was pregnant? Was it possible he had run from his responsibilities? Or had he never come back for some other reason?

"What was Jacob's last name?" Mary asked. Ruthanne sorted through the pieces in the puzzle box, shoving pieces aside randomly, and Mary wasn't sure if she knew what she was looking for now. She started to doubt Ruthanne was going to answer her, but then finally Ruthanne spoke.

"I don't remember," she said, and she looked up at Mary, her eyes sad. Mary felt her stomach turn. She'd seen that look on Mom's face many times as her disease had progressed, when she suddenly couldn't remember something she should have known. It had been heartbreaking to watch her struggle, because she knew that her memory was going. The fact that she knew what was going on and was powerless to stop it had made watching her health decline a thousand times worse. Mary said a quick prayer for Ruthanne, asking the Lord to bless her and comfort her, and, if it was His will, to spare what was left of her memory.

Mary wasn't sure she should push the older woman anymore, but finally decided it was worth at least asking. "Ruthanne, do you know anyone named Stuart? Stuart Hendricks?"

The woman shook her head. "That name doesn't sound familiar."

Mary slid her fingers over the photo on the table again. Ruthanne might not remember what happened to Jacob, but perhaps she could help Mary figure out the connection between Stuart and the newspaper clipping. Mary hadn't expected this visit to the tailor to yield so much information, and it couldn't hurt to ask a few more questions.

"I heard something about a robbery . . ." She let her voice trail off, but Ruthanne didn't volunteer any information, so she kept going. "A family with your last name was robbed."

Ruthanne shook her head, her eyes glazing over again as she stared at Mary like she'd forgotten why she was here. "What was your name again?"

"Mary — Mary Fisher."

"I'm pleased to make your acquaintance." She held out her hand, and Mary shook it. Ruthanne reached for another puzzle piece, seeming to find comfort in the simple act of putting the pieces together. Perhaps when her mind failed her, the familiarity and organization of a puzzle was all that made sense.

Ruthanne looked down at the picture again of Esther and Jacob. "What a handsome couple. Do you know them?"

Mary felt her stomach sink. Ruthanne was obviously confused. How much of what she'd said so far could Mary believe?

The elderly woman began to hum softly to herself, and Mary's gaze returned to her necklace. The emeralds sparkled, even in the muted sunlight. The front door chimed, and seconds later, a woman a few years younger than Mary popped her head into the doorway. She looked back and forth between the two women. She was petite and wore an old flannel shirt and jeans over her slim frame.

"Oh, I'm sorry," the woman said. "I had to step out and forgot to lock the door."

"It's no problem," Mary said as she stood up, reaching for her sweater on the hook behind the door. "You must be Teresa."

"I am. Teresa Porter." Teresa glanced at Ruthanne. "Did she tell you that?"

"She did. And she told me you were quite the seamstress."

"I'm not as good as she was. She started this shop when she was just a teenager, before she even got married. Can you believe that?"

Mary nodded. "She must have been quite entrepreneurial."

"She had to be, I guess. Anyway, I'm glad

Mom was able to speak to you. It comes and goes, you know."

Mary did know, all too well.

Teresa glanced at the sweater in Mary's hands. "Did you bring something for me to alter?"

"There's a tear in my sweater." Mary held out the sweater to show her where the seam was torn. "I hate to ask, but I wanted to see if it were possible for you to fix it today."

Teresa pulled it closer and fingered the material. "I usually schedule out a week ahead, but I suppose I could do it. But it won't be ready until later tonight."

Mary felt her shoulders unhitch. She would have the sweater to wear tomorrow, after all. "I can pick it up whenever you have it done."

A long breath slipped from Ruthanne's mouth, and when Mary looked back at her, the woman had fallen asleep leaning back in her chair. Teresa motioned Mary back into the other room, whispering, "We should let her rest. But come pick out what color thread you want me to use."

"Of course." Mary put the photo back in her handbag and before she followed Teresa back into the room with the sewing machines.

Teresa sat down at a small desk with a

sewing machine and gestured to a rack that displayed dozens of colors of thread. Mary zeroed in on the spools of blue thread and tried to decide between two shades of navy.

"You wouldn't believe how many people don't know how to sew a button on these days," Teresa said. She held the sleeve of Mary's sweater up against the two different spools.

"I guess it's good for business."

"That it is." Teresa nodded to several baskets with clothes in them. "There seems to be no shortage of missing buttons and long trousers in Ivy Bay."

Mary thought of the missing buttons and long slacks in her own closet that needed hemming. She kept thinking she would find time to sew, but the time never seemed to come. Perhaps she would need to make another run down to Willards' soon.

"I think this one matches nicely," Teresa said, pointing at the spool with a slightly warmer tint.

Mary nodded. "That looks good. Let's go with that one." She leaned in toward Teresa. "Your mother-in-law is wearing a beautiful necklace." She hoped she wasn't being too forward, but Teresa didn't seem to mind.

Teresa nodded as she pulled the spool off the display and began unraveling the thread.

"It's been in the Willard family for generations. She won't part with it and insists on wearing it all the time."

Mary tried to choose her words carefully. "I can understand that. I heard something about a robbery at her house when she was younger. Surely that would make someone afraid to leave valuables lying around."

"It was a rough time. I don't think she has ever really recovered." Teresa used tiny scissors to snip off a length of the thread and then wound the rest of the thread back around the spool. "And that makes sense, I guess. It totally changed her life."

"What do you mean?" Mary asked. She felt a bit nosy, but Teresa kept talking.

"They never found the person who broke in." She pulled a needle out of a package and threaded it expertly. "The Willards were already struggling financially, and the theft put them over the edge. They searched for years for the person who took their money and jewelry. It was big news for a long time, or at least, that's what I was told." Teresa laid the threaded needle down and turned to the sweater, fingering the hole, pulling the pieces together. "My husband still talks about it every once in a while, but Ruthanne doesn't talk about it anymore. My husband wonders what life would have been like for us if that money hadn't been taken. Ruth-anne's parents were able to keep the house until they moved into a retirement home, but that was the last big party there."

"I'm sorry to hear that they lost so much."

"I don't think Ruthanne was sorry, at least not in the long run. If the family hadn't been toppled off their high horse, so to speak, she would probably never have been permitted to marry Archie Porter. And she wouldn't have been able to open this shop, and all Mom ever wanted to do was sew. This business, along with her family and faith, meant everything to her."

"It sounds like she's lived a good, full life," Mary said gently.

Teresa nodded. "We sure love her."

"I can see that." Mary smiled. She could only hope her family would speak so kindly about her when she turned Ruthanne's age.

Teresa pulled the edges of the hole together one more time and then seemed satisfied. "I can make this so you won't even see it," she said. "I'll have it ready for you by seven."

"That sounds perfect." Mary turned toward the door.

"Thanks for spending some time with Mom. She doesn't get much company anymore."

"It was my pleasure." Mary thanked the woman and stepped out into the street, then walked briskly back to the car in the rain. As she opened her car door, Mary tried to sort through what she'd learned. Valuable jewelry had been taken from the Willards' house. And somehow Mom had ended up with a bracelet that matched Ruthanne's necklace. If her mother had had this bracelet since she was a teenager, why had she never shown it to her or Betty before? Why had she hidden it? But if Mom had known the bracelet was stolen, she wouldn't have kept it, would she? Could Jacob have been involved in the theft? Could a man with no money who had learned he was about to become a father find himself desperate enough to steal? What about Stuart Hendricks, whoever he was? Why did he save a clipping about the theft?

Mary didn't know what to believe, especially about Jacob. But then, she realized, aside from her mother's letters, she knew almost nothing about the man. As Mary walked back out to her car, she knew that she had to find out more about him. And she knew just where to find it.

FIFTEEN

Mary parked her car on Main Street near the bookshop and started walking toward the county clerk's office on Meeting House Road. As she walked, she pulled her phone out of her purse and called Betty. She asked Betty for the phone number for Amelia Shepard, Tabitha's granddaughter. She hoped Amelia would have some information about her grandmother's whereabouts.

"Hi, Amelia, this is Mary Fisher," Mary said when Amelia picked up. "How are you?"

"Well, hello, Mrs. Fisher," Amelia replied. "This is a pleasant surprise." Mary heard water running in the background, and she heard the voice of a child talking to her.

"I tried to visit your grandmother this morning, but no one answered the door. I was a little concerned."

"Oh, you are so kind to check on her. Dawn actually drove Grandma over to

Boston to visit my dad."

It was strange that Dawn didn't mention their trip when she saw her on Tuesday night.

"How lovely," Mary said, trying not to show her surprise. "When did they leave?"

"Yesterday," Amelia explained. "She's supposed to stay for a week, but you know how she hates the city. I'm guessing she'll be back in a day or two."

Mary wasn't sure if Tabitha had a cell phone, but Dawn must. But Mary was hesitant to ask. She had already made it clear she wanted to speak with Tabitha, and she didn't want to be pushy or spoil her time with her son.

"Well, I'm glad to hear she's doing all right. If you get a chance to talk with her, please say hi for me. I'm looking forward to seeing her when she gets back."

After Mary hung up with Amelia, she hurried to the county clerk's office. So much had happened in the past few days that it felt a bit overwhelming to her. The call from *Cape Cod Living.* The arrival of the Hartell books. The discovery of the letters, and Karly Sundin's strange behavior. Meeting Karen Rivers and Sally Parks and Ruthanne Willard. And now Tabitha had left town, knowing that Mary wanted to talk with her.

She hoped she would be able to find some answers today to help her make sense of it all.

The smell of old paper and musty books hit Mary as she stepped into the county clerk's office. She inhaled deeply. Some might find the odor stifling, but to Mary, it smelled like history mixed with adventure, and she took another whiff as she walked toward the counter, which was covered with copies of the *Ivy Bay Bugle* and notes from the last county selectmen's meeting. The room was crowded with filing cabinets and cupboards and smelled distinctly of aging paper.

Bea Winslow looked up from the magazine she was reading and smiled.

"You again?" Bea laughed. "You must be working on another mystery." She leaned back and rubbed her hands together.

"Of sorts," Mary said. She looked down at Bea's magazine. It was a running magazine, and Bea had it open to a spread that compared different kinds of running shoes. "Shopping for new shoes?" At seventy, Bea had more energy than most twenty-year-olds, and she liked to participate in all sorts of strenuous outdoor activities in her spare time. Mary enjoyed a walk on the beach now and then, but she was in awe of Bea's energy levels.

"I'm doing a 10K in a few weeks with my daughter and her kids," Bea said. Mary nodded. She'd met Bea's daughter, a nurse at a hospital in Hyannis, and Bea's two teenage granddaughters at a Memorial Day picnic in Albert Paddington Park. "I want to get some new kicks so I can beat them. We have a little wager going; the loser has to buy pizza for everyone after the race. So obviously I want to win."

"Naturally." Mary thought it was sweet that three generations of Winslows were exercising together. What a legacy of good health Bea was leaving for her family.

"What do you think? Can you see me in these?" Bea looked down over her reading glasses and pointed to a pair of shoes with hot-pink soles and fluorescent-yellow laces. "They're supposed to be quite good for people of my build."

The colors weren't Mary's taste, but then again, she supposed she probably wasn't the target market for the shoes. "I think you'll look good in whatever shoes you buy. And the color won't help you move any faster, anyway."

"Sure it will." Bea watched her, serious. "Everyone will be so confused at the horrible color combination on my feet that I'll

218

be able to blow right past them."

Mary laughed, and Bea put a Post-it on the page and closed the magazine. "So what can I help you find today?"

"I'm looking for information on a couple of men. Birth certificates, marriage licenses, property records, that sort of thing."

"From how long ago?"

Mary did some quick math in her head. "The birth certificates would probably be from the later 1920s. The other records would be later."

Bea nodded. "Then you want the computer over there." She pointed to an ancient computer terminal in the corner of the room, between a buckling bookshelf of leather-bound record books and a stack of dusty magazines almost as tall as Mary. Mary nodded and sat down in front of the computer. The gray plastic case was grubby with years of fingerprints, and the letters were worn off the keys. Mary shook the mouse gently to wake the screen.

"Now, let me see," Bea said, leaning in over Mary's shoulder to look at the screen. "There should be a program for searching birth and death records." She stared at the screen and muttered under her breath. Mary looked at the tabs on the top of the page, but none of them said "Birth Certificates."

"Megan set this up for me. She's quite the computer whiz, you know," Bea said proudly, referring to her younger granddaughter.

Mary knew that the budget was very tight, and a few years back when Bea started digitizing the county's records, there was no money to buy the software she needed. Megan, then only a freshman in high school, had created the program that allowed Bea to enter information from the old handwritten records into a database program. Now they were fully searchable, though Mary knew from past experience that it often took some work to get them there.

"If I could just remember how to do this . . ." She reached over Mary's arm and moved the mouse, clicking on a few links. None of them led to what looked like the database program she was looking for.

Mary knew that as young as Bea sometimes seemed, she was still something of a novice when it came to computers. She felt much more comfortable digging through boxes of old documents and registers.

"Let me call Megan," Bea finally said, and went back behind the counter. A minute later, she was back, and she had her phone cradled between her ear and her shoulder.

"Got it," she said, as she clicked in the right place and repeated the password Megan gave her. "Thanks, Meg." She laid the phone back on the counter and turned to Mary. "Thank goodness I called during lunch. If you'd come in during one of her classes, who knows when we'd have figured this out." She typed in the password, and they both watched as the ancient computer struggled to pull up the page. A moment later, a page popped up with search fields.

"There you go," Bea said. "You said you wanted to search birth records?"

Mary nodded, and Bea pointed to the place where she was supposed to click.

"Just put in the name here, and the date here."

"Great. Thank you so much."

"Let me know if I can be any more help," Bea said, and stepped back behind the desk. Mary wasn't sure how much help Bea really would be, but she appreciated the offer.

Mary rested her fingers on the keyboard and tried to figure out how to find what she was looking for. In the First Name field, she entered Jacob. She left the last name blank, and entered a date range of 1926–29. Then she hit Enter and prayed that something useful would pop up.

A list of a dozen Jacobs who had been born in Barnstable County in those years popped up. Jacob Wright Abel. Jacob W. Bremmerman III. Jacob S. Drew. Jacob David Lipschitz. Mary studied each name, hoping for the right name to jump out at her, but there was just no way to tell. Any of these could be her Jacob. And there was no guarantee that the man her mother had loved had been born in Cape Cod at all. Just in case, Mary hit the Print button, and a sheet of names and birth dates came out of the laser printer under the table.

Next, Mary entered the name Stuart Hendricks into the name field. She left the date range blank. She checked her phone while the computer loaded the results. No messages. Things must be going okay at the shop or Rebecca would have called. Finally, the computer spit out the results. No matches. Of course, Mary reminded herself, that didn't mean much. He could have been born elsewhere and moved to Cape Cod at some point.

Mary tapped her fingers lightly on the keys. There was no need to look up the next name that came to her. She knew all the details that should be on that birth certificate. But, then, what would it hurt to make sure? She would just check.

Mary looked around, as if someone might observe what she was about to do, but Bea was the only one in the room, and she was absorbed in her magazine. Slowly, carefully, Mary typed in the name Elizabeth Esther Nelson. She entered Betty's birthday too. She hit Enter and waited for Betty's birth certificate to load. One result came back. She clicked on it, and a scan of Betty's birth certificate appeared on her screen.

The certificate showed Betty's name, birth date, and weight. It listed Cape Cod Hospital as her place of birth. There were impressions of tiny little hands and feet. And the line for Father's Name read "Davis Nelson."

Mary sat back in her chair. Was it possible that Essy had known the truth but recorded the name of her husband, not Betty's real father, on the official document? Or had she simply listed the real facts? Mary moved the mouse around aimlessly. Once again, there was no way to know.

Mary clicked out of the birth certificate section and found her way to the property records section of the database. Mary wasn't sure how far back these records went. For really old records — centuries-old — Mary had had to dig around in the boxes stored in the basement or the records room in the past, and she hoped that wouldn't be necessary here. She typed in the address of the Rivers Accounting Firm building.

According to the records, the building was currently owned by Max and Karen Rivers. They had owned it for just over thirty years. That matched what Karen had told her. And . . . Mary scrolled down the page. They had bought the property from a Stuart Hendricks.

Mary shifted in the stiff wooden chair. So Stuart was indeed the artist who'd owned the building, and who had left behind the books and the news clipping about the robbery when he left. But what was his connection to Jacob, and to Essy?

Mary tapped her fingers on the keys. She searched for the records for each of the Jacobs on her list from earlier. This was going to take a while, and she tried to be patient while the program loaded each result. While some of the Jacobs had owned property in Barnstable County, none of them had owned anything in Ivy Bay.

She typed the first Jacob, Jacob Wright Abel, into the marriage records search field and waited while the program retrieved the results. It was slow, but it wasn't a bad program, especially for a high schooler to have designed. Megan no doubt had a bright future ahead of her.

Jacob Wright Abel, it turned out, had been married three times, and to two different women named Natalie. Well, that was strange luck. She supposed that must have made family reunions challenging. She laughed, imagining his family members mixing up his wives. But there was nothing that made her think this was her Jacob, so she moved on to the next name on her list. Jacob W. Bremmerman III had never been married, at least not in Barnstable County. She went through the list and came up with nothing.

This was hopeless. She wasn't getting any closer to finding answers, and she didn't know where else to look. In desperation, she entered one more name into the marriage certificate search. Stuart Hendricks. Mary glanced at Bea as she waited for it to load. Bea had finished with her magazine and moved onto filing paperwork in one of the many ancient filing cabinets in the packed room. Mary glanced back at the screen. Apparently, Stuart Drew Hendricks had gotten married, in 1952, to a Marghretta Alice Wood. Interesting. Drew was not an uncommon name, but . . . Mary scanned the rest of the certificate. Stuart Drew Hendricks was born May 21, 1926. Mary turned back to her list of Jacobs, and saw it, just like she remembered. Jacob S. Drew, born May 21, 1926.

It was too much to be a coincidence. Could *S* stand for Stuart? There was no way. It had to be — and yet, it couldn't.

She hit Print, and a copy of the marriage certificate slid smoothly out of the printer.

"Find anything?" Bea called as she straightened up and pushed in a drawer of a metal filing cabinet.

"Actually, I think I might have," Mary said without taking her eyes from the screen.

"Good!" Bea said. "Megan will be so glad to hear it!" She grabbed another file folder and pulled out the top drawer.

Mary grabbed the printout and looked it over, as if seeing it on paper would make it seem more real. And somehow, seeing it there in black and white, she suddenly felt sure of what she now realized she had begun to suspect: Jacob and Stuart were the same person.

Mary was still thinking through the ramifications of that when her cell phone beeped. She reached for her purse and dug it out quickly.

There was a short text from Rebecca that read: "Call me. ASAP."

She quickly dialed the shop's phone number, and Rebecca answered the phone, but her words were so muttered at first that Mary couldn't understand her. It sounded like she was about to cry. "What's wrong, Rebecca?"

There was a shuffling sound in the background, and a child called out. Mary heard a bang.

"Oh man," Rebecca said. "Hold on a sec."

Mary tried to wait patiently for Rebecca to return to the phone. What was happening in her bookshop? The door chimed in the background, and then Rebecca returned to the phone, sniffing before she talked. "It's terrible."

Thoughts of terrible raced through her mind. A fire. An injury. A lawsuit. Instead, she took a deep breath. "What happened?"

Rebecca gave a loud sigh. "I don't even know where to start."

"Are there any customers in the store?"

"Not anymore." She sighed again. "I think I scared them away."

Mary cast an apologetic glance at Bea, who held up a hand to wave Mary's concern away without looking up from the filing cabinet. "Why don't you start at the beginning?"

Rebecca took a deep breath. "Kaley Court came in with her dog to see if we had a book on training dogs. Little Pipp looked cute enough, even with his muddy paws, but the moment he saw Gus —"

Panic ripped through Mary. "Is Gus okay?"

"Oh yes, he's just dandy. He led Pipp on a chase that would have made Bugs Bunny proud. It took Kaley and I way too long to corral the two of them, and I wish we did have books on training for that little trouble-maker of hers, because she needs one."

Mary sighed. "How is the store?"

Rebecca cleared her throat.

"What's wrong, Rebecca?"

"There's mud — well, there's mud pretty much everywhere." She emphasized each syllable in the last word. "It's a disaster."

Mary took a deep breath. She tried to stay calm. "Don't worry about it. We'll just have to mop again tonight. It will be okay."

Rebecca didn't seem to hear her. "After Kaley left, I was trying to check a customer out, and I couldn't keep an eye on every-thing. There was this little boy, and I guess he was hanging on the picket fence or something. The gate, it broke right off."

Mary groaned at her words. She shouldn't have spent so much time searching for information today. She needed to be back at the shop, helping Rebecca prepare for their big day tomorrow. This mystery of her mother had been resting for almost seventy years now; it could certainly wait a few more days for resolution.

"I'm on my way back."

The front door chimed again.

"I gotta go," Rebecca whispered. "Can you please hurry?"

"I'll be there soon."

SIXTEEN

It had started raining again while Mary was in the county clerk's office, and thunder crackled overhead as she rushed back to the shop. She glanced at her watch as she walked down Meeting House Road. It was already twenty minutes after noon. Her hours spent on research seemed to slip away.

Mary rushed into the store and looked around. Oh dear. Rebecca hadn't been kidding when she said the bookshop was a disaster. There was mud streaked across the floor. Books were scattered in piles on shelves and tables, and the broken gate rested against the white picket fence. Mary leaned back against the wall and surveyed all the damage. She would be up half the night repairing and cleaning everything.

Even though the store was a mess, the persistent rain continued to send a steady stream of customers into the store, keeping her and Rebecca busy until she locked the front door at six. Rebecca stayed for another half hour, closing out the register for the day, and then Mary sent her home to make dinner for her family. Ever since Mary returned this afternoon, Rebecca had been on the verge of collapsing into a good cry, and Mary encouraged her to do so when she got home. After Rebecca left, Mary straightened up a few things, then drove over to Willards' to pick up her sweater. Perhaps Ruthanne would be lucid again, and Mary could ask her a few more questions about the theft. It could be in her more coherent moments that she might remember what had happened to Jacob after the war. Teresa and her dog were waiting for her inside the shop, but when Mary glanced at the small kitchen where she'd met Ruthanne Willard Porter earlier that day, the light was off.

"Mom's watching TV in the house." Teresa held out the sweater to show her the sleeve. "Does that look right?" she asked.

"It's perfect," Mary told her. "Thank you for sewing this so quickly."

"I'm glad to do it." Teresa flashed her a smile. "Though next time, a little more time would be helpful."

"Of course," Mary replied with a nod. She would bring a stack of her clothes over to

Teresa to mend soon. Maybe it would give her the opportunity to speak with Ruthanne again.

Mary paid and thanked the woman and then hurried back to the car to clean up the shop. When Mary got back to the store, she looked around in dismay. It might take all night to clean up Pipp's muddy trail through the store, and she didn't have the slightest idea how she would fix the gate. Gus was napping in front of the radiator.

"What about you, Gus? You ready to help?"

The lazy cat didn't even stir.

Mary sat down behind the counter and picked up the phone, and then put it down again. Things had been tense with Betty since she'd found the letters, and she had already done so much to help Mary clean up the shop the first time around. Would Betty be willing to help her now? Mary shook her head. She didn't know what else to do.

"Hi, Betty," she said when her sister answered. "What are you doing tonight?"

Betty was working on a blanket she was knitting for her granddaughter's birthday, but she readily agreed to come help. Mary was grateful and sorry she had doubted. Her older sister had always gone out of her way to help her. Just because things were now . . . different . . . it didn't mean anything had changed.

Mary got off the phone with Betty and called Henry. He agreed to come over right away and arrived about ten minutes later, carrying a toolbox in his hands.

Henry tipped his baseball cap as he walked into the shop. "I heard there was a damsel in distress around here."

"My gate is in some serious distress." Mary grinned, pointing at the picket fence. "Apparently, it went up against a four-year-old and lost the battle."

He examined the gate resting against the fence, making lots of *"hmm"* noises as he examined it. Then he pulled out his cell phone and winked at her. "I believe I can fix this, as long as Jimmy Shepard can find it in his heart to open up his shop for us tonight."

He stepped away from Mary as he spoke into his phone. "Hi, Jimmy. I've got a little favor to ask of you." Henry explained that he needed some supplies from the store, and though Jimmy was on his way home, he agreed to come back to his store and help Henry.

"You're a champ, Jim Shepard," Henry said into the phone. "I can meet you in front of the store."

He closed the phone and held it up like a torch. "Success."

She released the breath she'd been holding. "Thank you, Henry. You are my hero."

"Jimmy's shop keeps *Misty Horizon* afloat, and my wallet helps keep the hardware store in business."

Mary knew Henry's hard work really kept the boat afloat, but she wasn't going to complain about Jimmy. Tonight, he was her champion as well.

Henry hurried toward the door. "I'll be back in a jiff, and we'll get that gate fixed up for you."

Betty came into the store carrying more bottles of cleanser just as Henry was walking out.

"Thank you so much for coming," Mary said, rushing to the door to take the bottles out of her hand. "You don't know how much I appreciate it."

"It's not a problem," Betty said, but there was something stiff about her movements.

"Are you okay?" Mary asked. Betty nodded. She wasn't moving as though she was in pain, like she did when her arthritis flared up.

"Why don't you start mopping?" Betty said. "And I'll tackle those chairs."

"That sounds like a good plan."

They worked in silence for a few minutes, and the air hung heavy between them. Mary longed to tell her sister what she'd learned about Stuart and Jacob today, but Betty seemed to be stewing on something, and she wanted to give her sister the space to process things. She didn't want to bring up the touchy subject again if Betty wasn't ready to hear it. Mary tried to focus on getting the shop ready, but she couldn't stop thinking about the bracelet, about Ruthanne, and about Jacob and Stuart.

"You left quite early this morning," Betty finally said.

Even though she'd checked in after her trip to Tabitha's this morning, and again when she asked for Amelia's number, Mary hadn't shared anything about what she'd been up to either time. Mary suspected that's what Betty was really hinting at.

"I made several stops, looking for information about Jacob," Mary said tentatively. If Betty didn't want to talk about it, she could change the subject and leave it there.

"Where did you go?" Betty straightened one of the overstuffed chairs by the hearth and reached for one of the aqua pillows.

Mary watched her sister, trying to read her. Was she really asking Mary to share information about Jacob, or was she just being polite? Betty was turned away from her, so she couldn't read her face, but her posture was still stiff.

"I met a woman who knew Jacob when he was young," Mary said carefully. Betty hit the pillow, to fluff it up, Mary supposed.

"What did she say about him?" Betty kept fluffing the pillow.

"She said all the girls had crushes on him," Mary said.

Betty kept pounding at what at this point had to be the fluffiest pillow in Ivy Bay.

"And . . ." She hesitated. Even if Betty did want to hear some of what she'd learned, she probably didn't want to hear this. But she'd asked. "You know that bracelet we found in the attic?"

Betty turned to face Mary. Mary could see she was waiting for her to go on.

"The woman had a matching necklace. The bracelet was stolen, along with a lot of other jewelry and money, from her house when she was young. That was not long before Jacob disappeared."

Betty gasped. "Oh, Mary, you don't think . . ." She let her voice trail off. The truth was, Mary wasn't sure what to think, but it seemed strange that Stuart had kept the clipping unless he had some reason to be interested in the robbery. And if Jacob and Stuart were the same person, and Jacob had been in trouble, it did seem possible that Jacob had had something to do with the robbery. But she just shrugged.

"And I think Jacob changed his name to Stuart Hendricks at some point."

"Stuart Hendricks, as in the illustrator for those book covers?" Betty said. Mary had filled Betty in on what she'd learned last night.

"Exactly." Mary swiped her mop across the floor. "And Stuart Hendricks used to have a studio here in Ivy Bay, in the building where Rivers Accounting is. That's where the books came from. He left them there, along with a newspaper clipping about the robbery."

Betty was now twisting the pillow between her hands.

"Karen found the books and dropped them off here, not knowing what was inside."

"You covered a lot of territory today," Betty said. She looked a bit overwhelmed, but she also looked interested. Engaged.

"I did. But I still didn't get any closer to finding out what happened to Stuart, or Jacob, and whether he is —" Mary hesitated. "Whether what we suspect is true." She nodded at the pillow in Betty's hands. "I think that pillow is sufficiently fluffed."

Betty looked down at the pillow in her hands like she didn't know what it was. She set it down gently on the chair.

"So what are you going to do next?" Betty asked.

Mary hesitated. Betty had previously made it clear she didn't want Mary to find answers. But now she seemed almost anxious to learn more.

"I am going to see if I can track down Stuart," she said.

"And when you find him?"

Mary noticed that her sister hadn't said *if*. She had full confidence that Mary would find him.

"I will ask him if he's your father," Mary said simply. "If you're okay with that."

Betty lowered herself into the chair. "Yes," she said quietly. "I want to know." She clutched the pillow on her lap.

Mary leaned her mop against the wall and sat down in the other chair. "Are you sure?"

"I am. I wasn't at first, but" — she looked down at her hands — "I didn't want to even consider the possibility. It would change everything. But the more I think about it, the more I realize that if it is true, I need to know. Evan would want to know. It would

238

affect him too, and his children. And, you never know, Jacob might be . . ."

Mary waited for Betty to go on. Betty played with the fringe on the edge of the pillow, separating the strands and lining them up carefully.

"He could still be alive."

"You want to meet him," Mary said simply.

Betty nodded.

"I do too." She adjusted the pillow behind her. "I promise I'll do everything I can to find him, Betty."

"I know you will."

"It won't change anything, you know." That wasn't exactly what she meant to say, since she knew it would affect them both profoundly, but Betty seemed to understand what she meant.

"We'll always be sisters, no matter what," Betty said quietly.

Mary held out her hand, and Betty reached over and gave it a squeeze.

"There's one more thing we could do to find out if it's true," Mary said.

"The DNA test." Betty pulled her hand back and twisted the fringe around her finger.

"I don't know how long they take, but I think we would just need to send in some hair or something painless like that."

"Okay," Betty said. "Let's do it."

They sat in silence for a minute, Mary thinking about the change in her sister's attitude. God had been working on Betty's heart, and she hoped He would be at work in hers too as she kept up her search.

Henry walked back into the shop. "What are you two doing, sitting around?" He laughed. "We have a shop to clean."

"Just a little break." Mary pushed herself up and held out a hand to pull Betty to her feet. "Before that, we were working hard."

"Did you get what you need?" Betty asked.

Henry walked over to the children's nook and knelt down in front of the gate.

"I did indeed. That gate is no match for my drill or Jimmy's hinge."

"Sir Henry," Mary said with a laugh. "You're our knight in shining armor."

Henry plugged in his drill and began to work.

The quiet moment the sisters had shared had dissipated with Henry's arrival, but Mary didn't mind. Betty wanted her to find Jacob, and she would do whatever it took to keep her promise to her sister.

When Mary and Betty finished cleaning, the pair stood at the door for a few moments and admired their handiwork. The pine floorboards glistened in the lamplight, the books were neatly shelved, the bookcases were dusted, and the children's area looked clean again and comfortable. Betty's floral arrangements filled the room with a sweet fragrance. Henry had finished the gate an hour ago and had gone home, and the children's nook looked as good as new.

"It looks fabulous." Betty wrapped her scarf around her neck and pulled a matching hat over her ears. "You could eat off that floor now."

Mary nodded. "I'm afraid I'm going to get spoiled."

Thankfully, they hadn't had to stay up all night cleaning, but they were both exhausted from the work. It was after ten when they got home, and Mary set Gus's carrying case on the ground and opened the latch. He leapt out of the case and scurried toward the living room.

"Get some rest," Betty said after she closed the garage door.

"You too, Bets." Mary put the sweater on the table and set the carrying case in the garage. "You'll be there for the interview tomorrow, won't you?"

"Only if I won't be a distraction."

"You're never a distraction! Maybe they

can even take a picture of us together."

"Picture?" Another look of panic crossed Betty's face. "I haven't even thought about what to wear."

Mary ran her fingers through her short hair. "You have a closet full of beautiful clothes."

"But this is for *Cape Cod Living*."

"Why don't you wear your gray suit and pale-pink blouse with your new gray pumps?"

Betty shook her head. "Eleanor would be appalled if I wore gray in a photograph," she said, referring to her very proper sister-in-law.

"What about one of your oxford shirts and pressed pants?"

"That could work," Betty muttered. "Oh, I don't know. And I don't think I can figure it out tonight. I'll have to get up early tomorrow and go through my closet."

"Thank you for everything, Bets." She gave her sister a quick hug. "Sleep well."

As Betty closed her bedroom door on the first floor of their house, Mary pulled a white bowl out of a kitchen cabinet and scooped some ice cream into it. Even though she was exhausted, it would still take her a few minutes to unwind from the day. She thought through all that had happened today. Tomorrow, after the interview, she'd try to find out more about Stuart. Maybe she'd try the library again, now that she had a new name to research. And she needed to find out more about Karly. What did she know about those books that she wasn't telling?

She pulled the photo of her mom and Jacob she'd found in the attic out of her purse and stared at it. Her eyes traced the lines of his handsome face, and she studied the strong set of his jaw and the lively humor she could see in his eyes.

"I'll find you, Jacob," she said quietly, then placed her bowl in the sink and went upstairs to bed.

SEVENTEEN

Gus woke Mary up a good half hour before her alarm was set to ring, licking her face at first and then nuzzling against her shoulder and neck. Mary had had trouble falling asleep and had stayed up late reading. She had finally finished *The Cellar Door*. Lady Vincent had found her husband locked up in the basement, just as Mary suspected, and Inspector Deniau had been arrested and kicked off the police force. And then, as the clock edged past midnight, she had drifted off to sleep at last.

"It's not time to get up yet," she moaned as she scratched his neck. Gus didn't seem to care that it wasn't seven yet, nor did he care that the writer and photographer from *Cape Cod Living* were coming today for the interview. He was hungry and wasn't going to give up until she decided to do something about it.

With a big yawn, Mary slowly got out of

bed. She padded down the stairs and stopped by Betty's door, but there was no light streaming out from under it yet. She fed Gus a can of breakfast tuna along with a bowl of milk and then returned to Betty's room. There was still no sound, so she knocked lightly on the wood and then cracked the door. Betty was buried under the covers in her antique sleigh bed.

"You have to find something to wear," Mary reminded her.

Betty groaned and then tossed a pillow toward the door. "It's too early to get up."

"Not according to Gus."

Betty rolled over, pulling the blue down comforter over her head. "There's a good reason why I don't own a cat." Sunlight streamed in through light gray linen curtains on the window and bathed the sky-blue walls in a warm glow.

"Ah, but you do," Mary said playfully. "The photographer will be at the store soon, so up and at 'em."

This time, Betty sat up and reached for the glass of water she kept on her bedside table. "How long do we have?" She took a long, thirsty drink.

Mary glanced at the antique clock on her dresser. "Less than three hours."

Betty tossed back her comforter and

swung her legs to the floor. She straightened up and started to walk toward the bathroom. Mary went upstairs, and after she showered, she dressed in her white plush robe and hauled her blow-dryer, brush, and makeup bag down to Betty's bathroom to get ready for the interview. The two sisters stood at the sink, under the bright lights, as Mary blew her short hair dry and Betty rolled her honey-blonde hair in hot rollers. After Mary brushed out her hair, she put on some powder, blush, and plum-colored lipstick.

Mary tilted her head, posing in front of the mirror. "What do you think?"

Betty took a pin out of the side of her lips and put it through the roller. "You should add a little more blush so the camera doesn't make you look pale."

Mary checked both sides of her cheeks. "Are you sure?"

"Just a smidgen." Betty put in her last roller. "And I think you need to wear something besides a robe."

Mary turned toward Betty, posing in the mirror with her robe. "I don't know. I think this will be more memorable."

"A little too memorable." Betty laughed as she reached for an aerosol can. Without a word, she began spraying Mary's hair.

Mary waved her arms in front of her face. "What are you doing?"

Betty laughed. "Just adding a little hair spray to keep your hair put."

Mary backed toward the door, holding her arms out in front of her face. "That's going to make it crack."

She rushed away from the aerosol can and up to her bedroom, dressing in her newly repaired sweater over a white button-down and a pair of khakis, then stepped into a pair of pumps with one-inch heels. She went into the kitchen, where Betty was scrambling egg whites for both of them, and Mary poured two cups of coffee. Betty surveyed her outfit and then reached out and straightened Mary's collar. "You look just perfect."

Mary did a quick turn. "Are you sure?"

"Positive."

Betty was still wearing her blue satin robe and curlers, but Mary was certain her sister would appear at the bookstore later this morning in an elegant outfit of some sort. Even in her robe and curlers, Betty managed to look refined. Mary opened the refrigerator and removed a container of peach yogurt from the top shelf.

"I'm going to walk over to the shop in the next half hour or so," Mary explained as she scooped yogurt into a bowl. "Just in case

Harrison Greer comes early."

Betty eyed the cat that was tangling himself around Mary's ankles. "This rascal is coming to the shop today, isn't he?"

Mary leaned down and petted Gus under his chin. "Of course. He's a fixture."

"Now that I got some rest, I'm so excited I could just explode. It's like you're representing the entire town of Ivy Bay today."

She sighed. "That's a fairly big mandate."

"You'll do a great job, Mar."

She took a deep breath and thanked her sister. She was nervous, but she knew she was doing something that would benefit the entire town, and she couldn't be more proud about that.

Mary watched the minutes slowly click by on the wall clock in the bookshop. She'd arrived a little before nine, and it was only nine fifteen now. Gus was sitting upright on the round display table in the middle of the room, like he was ready to welcome visitors. The sky was scattered with clouds, but the morning sun slipped through the windows, making the coral walls and Betty's floral arrangements glow with warmth. She had found notes from several friends wishing her success at the interview when she got in this morning. She would do her best to represent the entire town well.

The aroma of coffee mixed with the smell of old leather and freshly baked bread from Sweet Susan's wafted through the store. Even though the photographer wouldn't be able to capture the smell, she hoped the magazine's readers would be able to sense it. She loved the charm of the decor and the old building that housed her books, and she hoped the readers of this story would enjoy her store as much as she did.

She still had a while before Harrison was supposed to arrive, and the waiting was driving her crazy. Eyeing the cubbyholes next to her chair, she pulled out the stack of Hartell books and put them on the counter by her computer. She then pulled her mother's letters out of her purse and laid them next to the books. She wished she could find the letters that Jacob had written to her mother, to see if they held any more clues, but she hadn't found anything in her mother's things.

Looking at the book covers, she wondered again about the man who designed them, the man her mother loved. Jacob S. Drew. Stuart Hendricks. If they really were the same person, why had Jacob changed his name? Mother must have known he'd changed it, since she had collected the books he'd worked on. Perhaps Jacob had mailed the books to Essy. The only person Mary could think of who probably knew the answer to her questions was Tabitha. She had been Essy's best friend. If anyone knew what had really happened, it would be her.

She opened one of the book covers again and closed it, imagining her mother doing the same thing in the closet of her bedroom at night after everyone was in bed. How many years had her mother longed for Jacob? She didn't want to think ill of Mom for collecting the books of the man she once loved, years after she married. Perhaps the books were just a sentimental reminder of her younger years.

Karen Rivers could have taken them to the dump or to Goodwill or to a neighbor who enjoyed reading old books, but she'd brought them here instead. Mary felt like divine providence had brought the books and letters home to her. She prayed softly that God would guide her. He was the only One who knew the secrets of the letters and of Jacob. If He wanted her to seek answers, she would do it, but she didn't want to open a door, a wound from the past, that He wanted to remain locked.

Then you will know the truth, and the truth

will set you free.

The words from the book of John soothed her mind. The truth about Jesus had already set her heart free, but perhaps the truth about her family's past would also set her free as well. Or maybe the freedom was for someone else.

About ten minutes after she'd taken the books out of the cubby, the front door chimed. Henry walked inside with a bouquet of flowers and a vase in his hands. "Good morning," he said. "I heard it was going to be a special day."

She tucked the books and the letters back under the counter and smiled at his warm welcome. "I sure hope so."

"I know you already have a couple of Betty's beautiful bouquets in here, but Misty used to say a woman could never have enough flowers."

Mary hopped up from the stool, taking his offering of a beautiful vase and bouquet. "You married a wise woman, Henry Woodrow."

"That I did." He smiled. "I'm still not quite sure why she married me, though."

"Because you're a kind, funny, dashing man who knows how to fix gates and buy a girl lovely flowers." She set the bouquet on the front counter and inched it forward and

251

then back. It looked perfect sitting right beside her old cash register.

"See, I've got you fooled too." He pushed up his sleeves of his sweatshirt. "The shop looks great. You and Betty must have been here late last night."

"Not too bad," she said. "But we were glad when it was finally done."

"You'll be glad when this photo shoot is over, won't you?"

She nodded. "Extremely."

Henry looked toward the back of the shop. "Is that coffee I smell?"

She moved around the counter, toward the back of the shop. "I think we both need a cup of it."

Rebecca arrived a few minutes early, dressed in a tan corduroy skirt, a dark green turtleneck, and a pair of fashionable brown boots. Then Betty came, dressed in beige slacks and a light blue oxford shirt with a navy blazer, carrying a bunch of fresh flowers. Mary knew her sister had tried to dress simply, but Betty still looked stylish. Mary admired her for it. Mary glanced back up at the clock. It was twelve minutes after ten.

"Didn't he say he'd be here at ten?" Betty asked.

Nodding, Mary took her cell phone out of

her purse to see if Harrison had called. He hadn't.

"You know these magazine writers," Rebecca said with a wave of her hand, like she was an expert on the topic. "They're always late."

Mary wasn't sure how many magazine writers Rebecca knew, but she didn't have the opportunity to ask because the door opened again. Mary recognized the man from his photo in *Cape Cod Living.* His head was shaved, and he wore a black turtleneck and skinny jeans.

She rushed forward, holding out her hand. "You must be Harrison Greer."

He wiped his hand on his jeans and then held it out to her. "And you're Mary Fisher."

She pointed over her shoulder, at the three people near the counter. "Mary and crew." She quickly introduced everyone.

Harrison nodded toward the small group. "It's good to have a crew."

"A blessing." She glanced out the window behind him. "Is your photographer with you?"

Harrison checked the face of his large black watch. "He should be here any minute."

"I'm not in a rush."

He sniffed the air like Henry had.

"Would you like a cup of coffee?" she asked.

He nodded. "Please."

"Cream and sugar?"

He shook his head in response. "Just black for me."

To match his turtleneck and pants, she thought. Before Mary could step toward the back room, Rebecca had scurried off to get Harrison's coffee.

"Should I close the shop for our interview?" Mary asked.

Harrison glanced around the room. "I don't think so. I'd like to get some pictures of people perusing the books. If it gets too crazy, maybe you can close for a half hour."

"It rarely gets too crazy this time of year." Mary directed him back to the two chairs in front of the fireplace. "Why don't we sit back here?"

"Perfect," he replied, checking his watch again. "I think I'm going to give a quick call to the photographer before we start, just to make sure he's not lost."

Mary nodded, though she wasn't sure how anyone could get lost in Ivy Bay. If they reached the beach, they simply turned around and came back through the small town. There were only a few streets in downtown Ivy Bay.

Harrison hit a button on his phone and ducked toward a bookshelf. She glanced over at Henry and Betty, and they both smiled back at her. Henry flashed her a quick thumbs-up. They would both love her even if she totally botched the interview, but it was nice to have a cheering section.

"What?" She heard Harrison exclaim into the phone. "No, that's not okay."

She glanced back again at Betty and saw the worried look return to her face.

"But we have to do it today," Harrison continued. "I've got to have the whole spread to the printer by Monday." He paused before he spoke again, even more aggravated. "I'm already working the entire weekend to get it done."

Mary stood in front of one of the upholstered chairs, watching the fire blaze. The gas flames leapt and danced. If this article didn't work out, she would have to be okay with that. Some people in town might be upset, but she knew God gave good gifts to His people. Sometimes He took what seemed like good gifts away as well for a reason they might not understand.

Rebecca was waiting with the coffee when Harrison turned. He took it from her outstretched hand with a terse nod. "I've got bad news," he said to Mary, though his words were loud enough to be heard by everyone in the room.

Mary stood up. "What is it?"

"The photographer I scheduled today was called off to a bigger job this morning. For some reason, he didn't think it necessary to call me with the news." Harrison didn't try to hide his disappointment. "I'm so sorry, Mary. Without a photographer, I don't think we'll make the deadline. So I don't know how we'll be able to feature your shop."

Mary's head began to spin. Of course, she was disappointed. Over the past week, she had grown excited about how this piece could positively impact many businesses in the town of Ivy Bay.

Then it hit her. Her gaze moved toward the window at the front of the store, and across the street. "What if you could find another photographer?"

He shook his head. "There's no way I can get a decent photographer out here this morning."

"Well, there may be a way, actually . . ." Mary nodded toward the window. "There's a photographer who works across the street. A really good photographer." Mary wasn't sure what to make of her, or what she knew about the books, but she did know that

Karly was a good photographer. Maybe this would be a good way to get more out of Karly *and* save the article. "I can see if she's available."

Harrison pressed his lips together. "I don't know —"

"Why don't you just look at her portfolio?"

The frown didn't leave his face. "I don't want anyone getting upset if it doesn't work out."

"We'll do our best." She glanced back over at Rebecca, Henry, and Betty, and her little crew nodded in agreement. "She works just across the street. Let's go see if she's around." Mary led Harrison out of the shop. They waited for two cars to pass, and then she led Harrison across the street, to the storefront of Gems and Antiques. She glanced into the window and searched for Karly. Her heart sank when she didn't see her. Perhaps she wasn't in today.

"Let's see if we can find her." Mary stepped toward the door, and Harrison held it open for her. The store was quiet when they walked inside. Jayne was sitting on her stool behind the counter.

"Well, hello," Jayne said with a wave. She hurried to their side and held out her hand. "You must be the writer from *Cape Cod Living.*"

Even as he shook Jayne's hand, Harrison seemed hesitant to respond. Mary guessed that he must get all sorts of requests from people to feature their businesses, and some people might hound him for a story.

"We were actually looking for Karly," Mary explained.

"Let me grab her for you."

A few minutes later, Karly rounded the corner by an old armoire, walking toward them. Her face was streaked with dust, and she wore holey jeans and old tennis shoes.

"Hello, Mary," she said, her voice friendly, but there was a bit of questioning in her tone as she brushed off the sleeves of her long-sleeve T-shirt. "Jayne said you wanted to speak with me."

Harrison eyed her, and then looked over at Mary warily. Mary ignored the hint of disdain in his eyes. "Do you happen to have your portfolio with you today?"

"I do." She tucked a few strands of hair back into her ponytail. "I carry it with me pretty much wherever I go."

"Very good." Mary introduced Harrison without making any promises for work. "He wondered if he could take a quick look at it."

She hesitated at first, looking back and forth between the two of them before she

258

agreed to get her pictures. "Let me grab it for you."

In seconds, Karly returned from her car and moved a stack of antique quilts off a table to place her portfolio on it. When she opened her portfolio for Harrison, Mary hovered beside him to look at the pictures as well. Harrison didn't make any sounds as he studied the photos, and Mary wondered for a moment if she'd been wrong, that Karly's pictures weren't as good as she thought.

Harrison turned the page, and Mary saw a photograph of a familiar brick barn with an elm tree in front of it. Behind it was the water. Mary blinked and stared again at the picture. One of the covers of her mother's books looked just like this. Mary wasn't an expert on barns. She supposed one could easily look much like another. But this one did seem very familiar.

Harrison moved on to the next page and landed on the photo of the old man with the craggy face squinting into the sunrise. He looked at it carefully, and Mary looked down at it again too. It really was quite striking. There was something sad about the old man's expression, even though you couldn't really see his eyes. He was —

Mary silently sucked in her breath. She'd seen this man before. She thought back to the photo she'd found in her mom's things, the one that had been taken on the beach. Last night when she'd looked at it, she'd noticed the strong jaw, the high cheekbones. Even through the changes the years had brought, she could see those here too. Her heart raced. She didn't know how she knew it, but she was certain: She was looking at a picture of Jacob.

"Did you take this recently?" Mary tried to keep her voice steady. She didn't want to give away to Karly that anything was strange, lest Karly get suspicious.

Karly looked at Mary. "A while ago," she said, then quickly turned the page.

Harrison continued to look at the photos of the following pages.

"It's a striking picture," Mary continued. "Who is the man in it? Do you know him?" Jacob was alive. Or had been, fairly recently, at least.

"No," Karly said quickly, shifting on her feet. "I don't know who he is. I just saw him when I was out shooting, and I took his picture."

Something about the way she said it made Mary sure she wasn't telling the truth. She'd lied to Mary before. But how did Karly know Jacob? And why did she want Mary to think she didn't?

"Are you sure?" Mary asked, tilting her head. "He looks familiar. I wonder if —"

"Okay." Harrison closed the book and handed it back to Karly as if he hadn't heard a word of what they had been saying. He eyed her for a moment, drumming his fingers together before he spoke. "I can't guarantee that we'll use your photography, but if you could take some pictures for us today, the magazine will pay you what we would have paid the photographer who didn't show."

Mary's focus jolted back to the feature, and she smiled. "So you'll be able to run the story?"

"If the pictures turn out," Harrison said, his tone hardly a vote of confidence.

Karly stood a little taller. "I'll take pictures you can use." She looked at her employer. "If it's okay with Jayne for me to leave, of course."

Jayne nodded. "It's quiet here anyway right now. Just don't be gone too long."

He studied her for another moment. "How long would it take for you to get your equipment together?"

"Fifty minutes." She paused, and Mary could imagine her mind was racing. "But I might be able to do it in forty."

"Perfect." Harrison breathed a sigh of

relief. "We'll finish before lunch."

Mary breathed with relief as well. If all went well, the magazine would be featuring her bookstore in January. She could nail down Karly after the interview.

EIGHTEEN

"Why did you decide to open a bookshop?" Harrison asked after Mary gave him a tour of the store. He was sitting beside Mary in the upholstered chair that had just hours ago been streaked with dirt. He held a tablet with notes he'd scribbled in their last half hour together, and his cell phone had morphed into a digital recorder, sitting on the table between them.

Mary brushed her hands over her pants, thinking back to the days of her childhood, when the highlight of her week was visiting the bookmobile. She had loved to pile the basket of her bicycle full. She'd liked everything about books. The stories, the feel of the covers in her hands, the smell of the paper, the adventures they would take her on when she opened their pages. She began to explain. "I've loved to read books my entire life, especially mysteries."

Harrison nodded his head like he understood.

"When I was a kid, we came to Cape Cod to visit my grandparents every summer. Both sets of grandparents lived here, and one of my grandmothers was blind, so I would sit on the porch and read to her," Mary continued. "She loved mysteries, and so I came to enjoy them too. When I got older, I knew I wanted to work with books. I worked as a librarian for many years, and then God brought me back to my favorite place in the world to open my own bookshop."

"Why is Ivy Bay your favorite place?" he asked.

She looked over Harrison's shoulder, at Rebecca, Henry, and Betty, who had been pretending to make conversation at the counter, but she knew they were really listening to the interview. "Well, it's home, in many ways. This is where I was born, and, like I said, where we spent summers when my sister Betty and I were young. And I love the people. You never meet a stranger in Ivy Bay. Even the guests here are treated like they're locals." She gestured to a group of people who had just come in the front door. Rebecca greeted them and asked what they were looking for, and she led them to the thriller section.

"And I love the beach. When you grow up near the ocean, the water calls you back to it. I savor my walks along the bay and love hearing the gentle lapping of the waves."

Harrison tapped his pen on the paper. "You said you were born here?"

She nodded. "My parents grew up here, and they met and married right here in Ivy Bay. I feel like this little town is a part of who I am, and I'm so grateful that God has given me this opportunity to call it my home now."

Even with all its unexpected surprises since she'd moved back, Ivy Bay had ingrained itself in her heart. Her grandparents had welcomed her when she was young, and now that she returned, her family's friends welcomed her back. She could no longer imagine living anyplace else but here.

"So you think you're here to stay?" Harrison asked.

She flashed another look at her crew at the counter. "Absolutely."

"I have one last question for you." He glanced to his left at the hundreds of books on her shelves. "Do you ever think you'll write a mystery of your own?"

A deep laugh bubbled out of her. "I've been trying to write my own mystery for a long time now. I've always appreciated a good mystery, but I appreciate one even more now that I'm attempting to write one. Someday, I might actually finish it."

"Fair enough." Harrison laughed as he turned off the voice recorder on his phone.

As he stood up, Harrison thanked Mary and then walked back over to the front counter to ask Betty and Rebecca a few questions while Henry refilled Harrison's cup of coffee. The door chimed, and Karly rolled a large black case into the bookshop and tucked it behind the counter. Mary welcomed her, and she took her camera out of the case and put a different lens on it as she turned toward Harrison. Harrison used Mary's computer and printed out some forms he needed her to sign, and Mary handed her a pen.

"Do you have a specific idea of what you want for your spread?"

"I want a picture of the children's nook," he directed, pointing at the reader area with the flowers. "Then we can get a couple of shots with Mary and me talking by the fire."

Karly unloaded small portable lights from her case and set them on the floor, behind the chairs. It took her a few minutes to angle them before she took the pictures for him.

Karly followed Harrison around for a

good fifteen minutes, taking pictures of what he wanted, and, Mary noticed, taking a few without his direction as well. Mary didn't particularly care which pictures the magazine used. She just hoped they ran the story.

The door chimed again, and an older man walked into the shop. When he eyed the photographer and all the people watching him, Mary realized he was about to bolt back out the door. She nudged Rebecca toward him. "Please tell him he can stay as long as he'd like."

In the next few minutes, four more customers entered the shop, perusing books and reading them in chairs as Karly took pictures. She showed them to Harrison in her viewfinder. Mary heard him both critiquing her pictures and complimenting them as they worked together. Mary offered to help a young mother and her daughter who was begging for a copy of *Pinkalicious.* In the midst of what was beginning to feel like chaos to her, Henry said he was scheduled to take someone out on a fishing trip for the afternoon, and she thanked him again for helping her prepare and bringing her flowers and cheering her on. She was blessed indeed by her friendships in Ivy Bay.

Harrison and Karly were conferring behind the counter. "I think we've got it," he said, and Mary breathed a sigh of relief. They might be able to run the story, after all.

"Great," Karly said and started packing up her equipment. "I'll head home now and get these downloaded, and then I'll send them on right away."

"Thanks so much, Karly," Mary said, walking up to the girl. "I really appreciate it."

"It was no problem," she said, but didn't look at Mary.

"Do you have a minute?" Mary said. "I have something I'd like to talk to you about."

"Actually, now is not great," Karly said as she zipped her camera into its carrying case. "I have to get these pictures to Harrison right away."

"This will only take a moment," Mary said.

Karly started to shake her head, but just then Harrison came up beside her.

"Mary," Harrison said, "I just need to fact-check a couple of things with you." He glanced at his watch. "I have to be on the road in ten minutes, so let's make this quick."

Mary glanced from Harrison to Karly, and

with a resigned sigh, back to Harrison.

"Sure," she said, pasting a smile on her face. As she answered questions for Harrison, Karly slipped out of her sight and out the door.

Harrison was barking at someone on his cell phone when he left the shop a little before noon. Mary waved a good-bye to him, and Rebecca helped their remaining customers. When the shop was finally quiet, Rebecca left for her lunch break, and Mary shuffled slowly back to the reading area. She collapsed into one of the comfy chairs, and she stretched her legs out in front of her. The warmth from the fireplace felt good against her back. Then she closed her eyes and rested in the quiet.

She was exhausted. She'd spent days preparing for the interview, and then she'd maintained as dignified as possible composure for almost two hours. And it all seemed to drain out of her the moment they all left. She closed her eyes, pressing her fingers against her temples. She didn't remember much of what she said, but she hoped her words made sense. If they didn't, she hoped Harrison would have the grace to put them into proper order before he printed them.

She felt herself falling to sleep, and a good

half hour passed when she woke again with a start. The store was empty, except for her. Had any customers come in while she was asleep? What would they think of her, slumped over, sleeping on the job like that? Mary pushed herself up and looked around. She hoped she hadn't missed out on any sales. Surely the bell over the door would have woken her . . . but then again, she had been in a deep sleep.

Mary made her way to the counter. She always felt disoriented after a daytime nap. That was part of why she didn't often drift off during the day. It always took her a few minutes to remember where she was and what she had been doing. She sat down behind the counter and shook her mouse to awaken her computer. Then she looked down at the counter. There was nothing there.

Mary thought back through everything she'd done this morning. Before Harrison arrived, she'd taken the Hartell books out of the cubby and her mother's letters out of her purse. She'd returned the books, but in her busyness, she couldn't remember if she'd put the letters back with them. She moved around the counter and checked by the computer, where she thought she'd left them. Then she crouched down to search the dark cubbies. The books were where she remembered putting them, but the letters were gone.

After kneeling down, she searched through the trash can in case someone tossed them by accident, but the letters weren't there either. She quickly scanned the bookshelves, but they were nowhere to be found, so she went into the back closet in case someone had moved them there. Nothing.

Panicked, she picked up the phone and dialed Rebecca's cell. Rebecca said she had seen the letters on the counter before the interview but hadn't noticed them afterward. When she called Betty, her sister said she hadn't seen them at all. Henry was out on his boat for the afternoon so she couldn't contact him. Had someone come in and taken them while she was asleep? Leaning back against the counter, she tried to replay the past hours. Someone could have come in and taken the letters while she was asleep. She didn't remember Harrison coming behind the counter, but Karly had been there several times, taking things out of her bag. Clearly, Karly wanted the books, but did she want the letters as well? Could that have been what she'd been after the whole time? But what could she possibly want with them? And had she wanted them enough to steal them?

When Rebecca returned from lunch, Mary hurried across the street to speak with Karly. Her feet and legs were exhausted, but a surge of adrenaline propelled her forward. Karly knew Jacob. Karly had wanted those letters. And now, after everything that had happened today, Mary had a suspicion that she knew why.

Jayne Tucker greeted her at the door, a bottle of glass cleaner in her hands and a roll of paper towels tucked under her arm. "How was the interview?" She sprayed a glass display case of gemstones, and the gems sparkled in the sunlight as she wiped it clean.

"A bit hectic at first, but everything seemed to go well in the end." She smiled, but her stomach was jumpy.

Jayne laughed. "I'm sure you did splendid."

Mary glanced around the store, but she didn't see Karly. "Thanks, Jayne. Has Karly come back yet?"

"No, she went home to download the pictures after the photo shoot and hasn't come back yet." Jayne checked her watch. "I was actually starting to get worried about her. I thought she'd be back before one."

"Do you happen to know where she lives?"

Jayne tilted her head. "Is everything okay?"

She nodded. "I'm sure it is. I just have a couple of questions for her."

Jayne moved on to cleaning a case filled with antique buttons and pins. "Not exactly, but it's someplace near Barnstable, I think. She used a post office box for her mailing address."

The last time Mary asked where Karly lived, the woman avoided her question. But Jayne had told her who Karly lived with.

"I'll ask her to call you when she returns," Jayne said. "Or if we're not too busy, she can just step over to your store."

"Thanks, Jayne."

The rest of the afternoon was a busy blur. Whenever Mary crossed by the front window, she'd look across the street to see if she could spot Karly, but there was no sign of the young woman. Karly didn't try to call her, nor did she visit the bookshop.

At six, Mary and Rebecca closed the shop, and she stepped out onto the quiet street. Mary glanced across the street. Gems and Antiques was dark, as were most of the other stores. She sighed. Karly was avoiding her.

Mary would just have to track her down.

■ ■ ■ ■

When she opened the front door of her house, she set Gus down, and he ran off into the living room. She walked into the kitchen, where Betty was making a meal of chicken cacciatore and green beans. It smelled delicious, and Mary inhaled deeply and leaned back against the counter.

"How was the rest of your day?" she asked. "Did you have another meeting about the food drive this afternoon?"

Betty nodded. "We've got almost everything ready to start taking collections this Sunday. The only thing I have left to do is to stop by and talk to Tabitha Krause. She is going to donate some money to cover the cost of transporting the food to the shelter."

"Tabitha?" Mary took two plates out of the cabinet and set them on the counter. "Amelia told me she was in Boston, visiting her son." Mary moved the plates to the table and took down glasses.

Betty set the chicken dish on the table and began to serve out portions. "Dawn called me this afternoon. She said they were coming back tomorrow."

"She did?"

"I take it that she hasn't gotten back to

you yet?" Betty said, dishing out a steaming piece of chicken on Mary's plate.

"No, she hasn't," Mary said. She filled the glasses with water and set the salt and pepper shakers on the table.

"That's strange." Betty sat down, and Mary said a blessing, and they both started eating, but Mary's mind was whirring. "Did you ever find those letters?"

"No," Mary said as Betty cut a green bean in half. "Somehow, Mom's letters disappeared from the store."

"But who would have taken them?" Betty took a bite and chewed nervously.

Mary shook her head. "The only one that makes sense is Karly."

"Karly? But she seems like such a nice girl. Are you sure?"

Mary looked back down at her chicken and green beans. She'd been wrong before, thinking someone who must be innocent was the guilty party and that the guilty party was innocent, but she was almost sure that Karly was guilty in this case.

"I don't know for certain, but she was the only one there today who has asked repeatedly about the books," Mary replied. "I went over to Gems and Antiques to speak with Karly this afternoon, but she hadn't returned from lunch. Jayne said she would

have her call me, but I haven't heard anything yet."

"Well . . . ," Betty said, laying down her
fork. "Obviously we want them back. But
maybe it's not the end of the world. We
know what they said, right?"

Mary had read that last letter so many
times she could probably recite it verbatim.
And she had the scans she'd made. She
nodded reluctantly.

"We don't need the letters to look into
Jacob and Mom's relationship. I did some
research this afternoon on DNA tests."

"Oh?" Mary picked at the chicken with
her fork. She was glad Betty was finally
interested in finding out the truth, but as
she thought through all that had happened
today, Mary just kept coming up with more
questions.

"There's a kit you can order online.
They'll deliver it to you, and then you send
it back, and it only takes a week to get the
results. If Dad was really my father as well
as yours, our DNA will match closely, and
if it doesn't, well . . . then we'll know."

Mary nodded, but she was distracted. She
was thinking through the other letters,
replaying them in her mind, trying to
remember what they said.

"I wanted to check with you before I

ordered the kit. Do you think that will be good enough? There are also clinics where we could go and get the test done."

Mary thought through the wording in the last letter again. It certainly did seem like it pointed to one specific answer. But what if she'd been reading it wrong all along? What if her mom had been talking about something else entirely in that letter?

Suddenly, it all clicked. She couldn't believe she hadn't seen it before.

"Mary?" Betty asked. "What do you think? About the test?"

"Let's hold off on the test," Mary said. "I think I know what happened to Jacob."

Nineteen

Saturday morning, Mary drove back to Tabitha's house. She could see lights on inside the house, and she could see someone moving around through an upstairs window. The door of the detached garage on the side of the house was open, and Mary could see Tabitha's car inside. They were home. She knocked on the door and waited. She heard footsteps inside. Mary's car was parked at the curb outside the house, but even without that, there could not be much question about who was at the door. Tabitha might have been avoiding her, but Mary was not leaving here without answers.

The door swung open. Dawn did not seem surprised to see Mary standing there. She gestured for Mary to step inside. "You'd better come in," she said. She was friendly as always, but something about her manner felt reserved.

"I'm so glad you're home. I have been trying to get hold of you for days," Mary said as gently as she could. "I was starting to get worried."

"Tabitha needed a little time," Dawn said simply. "She's been wanting to see you, but some things are hard for her to talk about," Dawn tried to explain. "I'll let her tell you the story, though." She led Mary into the parlor and pointed to a brocade love seat by the window. "Have a seat. Tabitha is just finishing getting ready. She will be right down. Can I get you anything?"

"No, thanks. I'm okay," Mary said.

"I just brewed a fresh pot of coffee for Tabitha. It wouldn't be any trouble," Dawn said knowingly, and Mary relented.

"That would be lovely," Mary said. Dawn disappeared into the kitchen, and Mary was left alone in the parlor. The high-ceilinged room was lovely, with rich velvet draperies and a thick Persian rug and beautiful Queen Anne furniture. There was an intricately carved upright piano in the corner. Mary remembered Tabitha playing concerts in this room when she was younger.

There was a noise on the stairs, and Mary looked up to see Tabitha clutching the banister, coming down the steps one at a time. She was wearing a slate-gray turtle-neck and black pants, her silver hair pulled back in a neat bun, and she had her cane and a cardboard box tucked under her arm.

"Hello, Mary," Tabitha said. Mary stood up and moved toward the staircase to help her down, but Tabitha waved her away. "I can make it. I'm not *that* old yet."

Mary felt like a child again, and she sat down. "You look lovely, as always," she said, and Tabitha nodded and stepped off the bottom step and shuffled across the floor. Tabitha's health was good, but her back was stooped and she moved slowly. Finally, Tabitha sat down on the toile armchair across from Mary.

"So. You've come to see me," Tabitha said and gave Mary a smile. She placed the wooden box on the low mahogany coffee table in front of her.

"Yes," Mary said. "I have a few questions for you."

"I thought you might." Tabitha sighed. "When I heard you'd found Essy's letters, I knew you'd be coming around here with questions. I hoped you'd drop it if I stayed away. Essy never would have wanted you to see those letters. But I should have known that you wouldn't just forget like that." She crossed her thin legs. "So it's probably best to just get it all out into the open. Go ahead."

Mary leaned forward. "Do you know where Jacob is?" she said.

Tabitha laughed. "Well, you don't like to ease into things, do you?"

"No, I don't — it's just that, it's very important that I find him." Here, Tabitha had her all flustered like she was a child again.

"Is it now?" Tabitha's eyebrow arched. "And why is that?"

Dawn came back into the room carrying a silver tray and two teacups. She set a cup down on the coffee table in front of each of them, then set a bowl of sugar and a pitcher of cream between them and added a plate of biscotti and some paper napkins. Mary was glad for the distraction, and she waited until Dawn had left the room again to answer.

"Because my mother loved him, didn't she?"

Tabitha watched Mary for a moment, then picked up a silver spoon and shoveled sugar into her cup. Mary could see that her hands were shaking.

"Yes, she did. Very much." Tabitha smiled, as if at a far-off memory. "Essy and I met Jacob a long time ago, at a dance at the old pavilion here in Ivy Bay. He strolled right up to Essy and told her how beautiful she was. And she was beautiful; there was no doubt about it. Jacob was smitten, and looking back, I think it was love at first sight for your mama too."

Mary took a piece of the almond biscotti from the plate and put it in a napkin. She was glad to hear that Jacob had cared for her mother like she had cared for him.

"And she began to write him," Mary prodded.

Tabitha nodded. "And he wrote her too, a letter a day sometimes. It was all hush-hush, of course, so her stepdad wouldn't find out. Jacob sent the letters to me, and I would deliver them to Essy."

Mary imagined the two young ladies, sneaking around with their letters so Grandfather Franklin wouldn't find out about it. Knowing her mother, she probably saw it as an adventure of sorts.

"But they couldn't be together."

"No." Tabitha stopped stirring and laid the spoon down gently. "But you already knew all that. What did you really come here to ask me?"

Mary hesitated. Verbalizing what she feared with Tabitha seemed so much more scary than it had been when she'd been talking to Betty.

"Is Betty Jacob's child?"

"No, of course not." Tabitha raised her trembling hands and took a sip of the coffee. "She's Davis's child, through and through."

Mary let out a heavy breath she hadn't realized she'd been holding. She'd figured all this out last night. But she'd also figured out that if the last letter, the one that talked about something bad they had done, wasn't referring to a child conceived out of wedlock, it referred to something far worse.

"I wasn't sure. At first, I thought —"

Tabitha nodded. "A lot of people did. He went away, and then your mother met Davis, and they married so quickly. And then, Betty was born so soon. Of course people wondered. But the truth is, what happened with Jacob . . . it changed her."

Mary struggled to figure out how to ask if Tabitha meant what she feared she did.

"They robbed the Willards, didn't they?"

Tabitha nodded. "Jacob was the one who broke into the safe. Your mother didn't actually steal anything. But she waited outside in the car and kept the engine running, and that was how they were able to leave before anyone could catch Jacob."

Mary stared down at her hands. It was what she had suspected, but it was still hard to hear the truth. Her mother had committed a robbery. Helped commit a robbery, anyway.

"Your mother was young and impetuous. She was always carefree, always doing exactly what pleased her at the moment."

Mary put the rest of the biscotti on her saucer. She had a lot of wonderful, fond memories of her mother, but she didn't know if she would describe Mom as passionate. She had always been calm, thoughtful, and strong willed in Mary's memory. She was kind and enjoyed beauty, but Mary only saw that flicker of passion every once in a while, usually when her mother was dancing. Then she was like another woman. It was almost as if she were stolen away by the magic and movement of the music. "That was what I loved about her. She knew how to make every moment count."

"But after Jacob, that changed?" Mary said.

"She realized what she'd done was wrong. She grew up after that. And then, as soon as your mom met Davis, all other boys seemed just like that — boys. Davis was a man. She fell hard for him, and she knew he was the one. She put all that nonsense behind her and married him."

"So she did love him?"

"Madly." Tabitha took a sip of her coffee

and leaned back against the chair. "Your mother never did anything halfway." She let out a laugh. "He'd just come back from the war, a hero for rescuing several fellow soldiers from the Germans. His father was a local judge, and Davis went to Ivy Bay High, so Essy had seen him when she was younger and admired him from afar. After a parade, he stopped one of his buddies and asked who that —"

"Gorgeous girl in the lilac dress was," Mary repeated the familiar words with her. This was one story she'd heard many times.

Tabitha smiled. "His buddy secured him an introduction, and later Davis introduced me to his buddy Walter Krause. We married a few days before Davis and Essy."

"And you all lived happily ever after."

"We weren't happy all the time, but we lived together through it all — mistakes, forgiveness, births, deaths, and sickness. And in the end, my Walter and I, we loved each other with all our hearts. And so did Davis and Essy. God gave both Essy and I men who loved us, and we sure loved them."

"I'm so glad." Mary had also been blessed with a happy marriage and a wonderful, loving family, and she was glad her mother had had the same, especially after the hard times that led up to it.

"Here." Tabitha set down her cup and handed Mary the wooden box. "Your mama left these with me a long time ago. She didn't want to hurt your father by keeping them in the house any longer, but she couldn't find it in herself to throw them away either."

Mary opened the box and saw a familiar stack of books. She lifted out the top book and saw the mystery with the lighthouse on it. The next book was the one with the brick barn. She flipped open the front cover and saw her mother's familiar bookplate on the inside. There were six books in the box, and not all of them were the same books she'd found outside her shop, but several of them were familiar. "You had Mom's copies of these books all along?"

"For the past forty years or so."

"Did she give you the letters from Jacob as well?"

Tabitha shook her head. "I'm afraid she got rid of those long before she gave me the books. She didn't want your daddy finding them. She knew they would only hurt him."

Mary looked down at the stack of books in her hand, reminders of her first love that she'd hidden to protect the man who had stood by her the rest of her life.

Dawn gave a light knock on the door

frame and then peeked her head around the corner. "Amelia's on the phone," she said. "She wants to know if she can call Mrs. Fisher to let her know that you're home from Boston."

The women laughed.

"You tell her thank you, but she doesn't have to call Mary. We're already having a fine time today." She turned to Mary. "Aren't we?"

Mary heartily agreed. She wanted to hear more about the happy times, about how wonderfully her mother's life had turned out. But she needed answers from Tabitha about what happened before that, about what she and Jacob had done. When Dawn stepped away, Mary tried to figure out how to ask what she needed to know. "But, Tabitha, did she and Jacob . . ." She paused and struggled to find the words to say what she was thinking.

"You have to remember that she thought they were doing something good. His sister was sick, and this was the only way they could think of to help her. Jacob sold the jewelry, and he used that and the cash to get her treatment. It saved her life."

Mary tried to find a way that it made sense, but she couldn't. "But afterward, when she realized what they'd done was wrong, why didn't she confess, try to make amends?"

Tabitha shook her head. "I guess we'll never know for sure. Probably, she thought it was old news, that it would only cause more hurt. Think about how many lives would have been affected if she'd confessed. Yours, certainly." Mary nodded. "And Jacob was off in the army. And the money was already gone. Patty was getting the treatment she needed."

It still didn't make total sense to Mary, but she tried to remember that her mother had been young, and that the woman who had raised her was not the same girl who would have done — had done — anything for love.

But that didn't mean Mary couldn't make amends herself. Now that she knew the truth, she would. Years ago, her mother had helped Jacob rob the Willards' house, and now Mary would do what she could to fix it. But there was one thing she had to do first.

TWENTY

Mary drove to the shop to open up for the day and found a parking spot in front of Meeting House Grocers. Karly's blue VW Bug was parked on the street as well. Mary walked past Gems and Antiques on the way to her shop, and she looked in the window of the antique store. Karly was inside, getting the register ready for the day. If Karly noticed her out of the corner of her eye, she didn't acknowledge her, but Mary stood at the window until Karly turned toward the glass. Mary waved, but instead of returning her wave, Karly looked away quickly, like she'd done something wrong.

Irritation flared inside her. Karly had taken something very valuable from her. She could walk inside and confront Karly today, but the young woman would probably stonewall her in front of the Tuckers. She would have to think of a better way to approach her.

Turning, she crossed the street, and as she walked, her frustration bubbled into anger. Perhaps Karly thought Mary wouldn't be able to prove that she'd stolen the letters so there was no reason for her to be worried. In her heart, she wanted to believe the best about Karly, but she was beginning to wonder if she should warn the Tuckers that there might be a whole lot more to the woman's story.

Rebecca was busy placing an Internet order into a box when Mary walked into the shop.

"Tabitha says to tell you hello," Mary said as she slung her jacket over the stool. "She called you Little Becky."

Rebecca curled a strand of hair behind her ear. "She calls everyone little. Which is funny, because she's tiny."

"Maybe it's her way of feeling bigger." Mary laughed. She sat down behind the counter. "I have a favor to ask you."

Rebecca turned back toward her. "Sure. What do you need?"

"Could you please call Jayne and ask her what time they're closing tonight?" Mary knew the Tuckers usually closed at six, just like Mary, but sometimes they closed earlier or later, depending on what else was going on in their lives. That was the benefit of owning your own business.

Rebecca picked up the telephone. "On your behalf?"

"No, just from an interested customer." Rebecca's eyebrows arched, but she didn't ask any more questions as she dialed the phone.

Mary slipped into the back to check on Gus, whom she'd dropped off before heading to Tabitha's. He was curled up asleep on one of the armchairs by the fire. Part of her wished she could curl up in the other chair and take a nap as well, but even if she did, she wouldn't be able to sleep. She had too many thoughts racing through her head.

When she walked back onto the main floor, Rebecca was hanging up the telephone. "Jayne said they're closing at five thirty."

She thought for a moment. "I think we'll close at five o'clock tonight."

Rebecca flashed her that questioning look again. "Are you going to tell me what's going on?"

Mary picked up a stack of books from a table and started to shelve them as she told Rebecca her plan.

A few hours later, she tried to explain her idea to Betty as well, but her sister looked at her like she was crazy. Betty reached for a bowl as she unloaded the dishwasher. "Karly's going to recognize you."

"She doesn't have any idea what car I drive."

Betty stacked two bowls together. "No, but she knows what you look like."

Mary sighed as she dried off the plates and set them in the cabinet. "We'll figure it out," she said with more confidence than she felt. But how hard could it really be to follow someone home? People in the books and movies tailed a suspect all the time. As long as Mary and Betty didn't get too close to her car, Karly would have no idea they were following her.

Betty closed the dishwasher and leaned back against it. "You're serious about this, aren't you?"

Mary nodded. "I have to find her grandfather, and I want to know if she has my letters as well."

"You're nuts."

"Possibly. But are you going to help me or not?"

Betty stepped toward the doorway. "I'll be right back."

Mary sat on a chair, and Gus jumped in her lap to keep her company while they waited for Betty. "You don't think I'm crazy, do you?" she asked as she scratched him behind his ears. He purred in response. Betty returned a few minutes later with a small bag packed full of accessories. She handed Mary a pair of large black sunglasses and a red cap that covered most of her hair.

"It's not cold enough for a hat," Mary protested with a wave.

"It is now." Betty laughed. "It will keep Karly from recognizing you."

Mary finally complied and donned the cap and sunglasses. Betty wore her wide-brimmed straw hat. It was a little before five thirty when Mary got into her car. Betty got in the passenger side a moment later, carrying two steaming travel mugs of coffee.

"We're not going to be out here all night," Mary said.

"It's better to be prepared." Betty sniffed and slipped them into the holders. Mary was glad she brought drinks. She didn't know quite how long this adventure would take. She started the ignition, and they drove up Shore Drive and onto Main Street. Karly's Volkswagen was still parked in front of Gems and Antiques.

Betty pulled her hat low on her forehead. She'd added a brown scarf to the mix and wrapped it over her chin and neck so most of her face was covered. "What do we do now?" she asked, her voice hushed.

Mary drove quickly down Main Street and turned onto Meeting House Road. "We'll wait for her right outside Ivy Bay, on one of those small roads that lead to the highway. When we see her drive by, we'll follow her."

"Are you sure she doesn't know what you drive?" Betty asked again.

"As sure as I can be."

Mary turned the car around on a side road, facing out to the highway so they could watch for Karly to pass. Betty pulled a small notepad and pen out of her purse.

"What are you doing?"

"I'm going to jot down every place we turn," Betty explained. "So we can find her house again . . . and if necessary, find our way home."

Mary straightened her scarf. "You know your smartphone has a GPS, right? You can just drop a pin when we get there, and it will tell us how to get home and allow us to find our way back."

"Drop a what?" Betty pulled her phone out of her purse and stared at the screen. Her son Evan had bought her the phone for Mother's Day, but she didn't have the slightest idea how to use it aside from making phone calls.

"Never mind. Paper works fine too."

Betty nodded and put the phone away.

"And the disguises were a great idea," Mary said.

She hoped it would be worth it. Mary took her tall cup from the holder, and as she sipped the coffee, she told her sister all that Tabitha had said. Betty leaned her head back against the seat. "Life would have been so different for all of us if Mom and Dad hadn't married."

She tilted her head. "Like we wouldn't even exist."

"For starters, yes." Betty chuckled. "And second, I don't think Mom would have been very happy with this Jacob, not if what Tabitha said is true. Dad was always honorable and completely devoted to her."

A blue car blew by them on the highway.

Betty leaned forward, trying to see around the corner house. "I think that was Karly, going way faster than she should."

Mary crept the car up to the road. The car was too far in the distance for her to figure out if it was a Volkswagen Bug or something else.

Betty looked over at her. "I think you should chance it."

"If it's not her car, we're doing this again tomorrow night."

"Tomorrow is Sunday."

"The next day, then," Mary said.

Betty nodded. "Fair enough."

Mary turned right onto the highway and slammed her foot on the pedal, as far down as it would go. Still, as the minutes passed, they were nowhere close to catching up with the blue flash of a car ahead of them.

"You're going to get a speeding ticket," Betty insisted.

"I can explain what we're doing."

"Officer," Betty mimicked, "it's an emergency. We're chasing a car because the woman might be the granddaughter of our mother's long-lost love from seventy years ago."

Mary laughed at her sister's imitation. "Okay," she finally admitted. "It wouldn't help much."

But she was still willing to risk it. Mary squinted her eyes, trying to see clearly through the sunglasses at dusk. They were catching up with a blue vehicle that could indeed be a Volkswagen.

Betty clapped her hands. "I think that's her."

Mary hit her brake pedal and hung back several car lengths. There were several cars in her rearview mirror but no cars between her and the Volkswagen. She hoped Karly didn't study her mirror too closely. They must look odd with their hats and sunglasses so late on a cloudy day, but Betty was right. Karly would have recognized them right away in her rearview mirror if they didn't have some sort of disguise.

About two miles past Barnstable, the Volkswagen's left turn signal flickered as Karly pulled into the left lane. Mary waited a brief moment and did the same thing.

"Left on Grayson," Mary told her sister, and Betty jotted down the name of the road and the direction after they turned.

They'd entered a middle-income beach community with quaint bungalows and elm trees that canopied postage stamp-sized lawns. Most of the cottages, Mary figured, were only occupied on the weekend, and she was glad that today was Saturday. Hopefully, Karly wouldn't notice a car she didn't recognize following her into the neighborhood. Mary still drove slowly, hanging back behind Karly so she wouldn't wonder at their vehicle, but not too far behind so she wouldn't lose her. She cracked the window and felt the cool breeze blowing off the bay. It smelled like burning wood out here near the beach, salty air mixed with the scent of the scrub pine trees.

They followed Karly's car to the right

before they doglegged again, and then straightened on a narrow road lined with red cedars. Mary called out the name of the streets with every turn, and she grew more worried as the seconds passed. If Karly didn't reach her destination soon, she would surely begin to wonder at the Impala following her out to a remote area along the beach.

The last turn Karly took was a left, into a long lane. Mary pulled to the side of the road.

Betty leaned forward, looking at the solitary mailbox at the end of the road. "It looks like a driveway."

Mary waited until Karly's taillights vanished, and then she pulled close to the drive. The end of the lane was obscured by pine trees mixed with aspens.

"What do we do now?" Betty asked.

Mary turned the wheel and pressed her foot gently against the gas pedal.

"We follow her."

Twenty-One

There was only one house at the end of the lane, and it had a beautiful view of the beach and bay. Karly's Volkswagen was parked in the driveway, and Mary could see her walking toward what looked like a garage a little ways from the house. Mary stared at the ramshackle house for a few seconds. It was an old, plain one-story home that desperately needed a coat of paint. A simple porch wound around the side of it, and a detached garage sat empty among the overgrown weeds and grass. About three hundred yards behind the tangled jungle of a backyard was a beautiful view of the bay.

She couldn't help but compare the home to the last beach house she'd visited, the exotic residence of Sally Parks, with its fountain and gate and endless rooms that spilled over the dunes.

Together, the women climbed out of the car and walked across the gravel toward the front door.

"She went that way," Betty said, pointing toward the garage.

"We'll talk to her later."

The two cement steps that led up to the porch were cracked, and the door hung askew.

Mary took a deep breath and then knocked. Seconds passed, and when no one answered, she tried the doorbell. She expected to hear it ring out, but it didn't seem to be working, so she knocked again.

"Perhaps Karly lives here by herself, after all," Betty suggested.

Mary craned her neck to see into the wide picture window on the other side of the door. She wasn't sure what to expect, perhaps a living room that was as neglected as the exterior walls, but the inside of the house looked neat and clean. There was a tan couch with pale-blue pillows and an armchair on each side of it. There were two lamps in the room, one of them on, and an opened newspaper on the coffee table.

She twisted the knob on the front door and it opened.

"Hello," she called out. "Is anyone home?"

When no one answered, she stepped into the front room.

"I wouldn't think a single girl would leave

her door unlocked," Betty said as she followed Mary inside.

"Hello?" Mary called again.

When no one answered, she walked tentatively into the kitchen. The refrigerator and dishwasher were an olive-green color and the linoleum was cracked, but the counters and table were cleared and wiped down. In spite of the old facade on this house, someone still cared for the inside.

Betty placed her hand on Mary's shoulder. "We should probably go."

Mary nodded. "In just a moment."

There was a screen door in front of her, leading to a sunporch filled with white wicker furniture, which had been covered with a pastel floral pattern. The screen was torn in multiple places, and the material on the furniture was faded, but in the distance was the beautiful view of the bay . . . and a large brick barn with an elm tree in front of it. It was the barn from Stuart's book cover and Karly's photograph.

She stepped out onto a faded rug on the porch. "Is anyone out here?" she called.

This time, someone answered her.

"I'm right back here," a man's voice replied. It sounded like he was outside, to the left of the porch. "Who's here?"

Mary opened the door of the sunporch

and stepped outside onto a large patio of cracked cement. There were two chairs and a plastic table against the house, and beyond that, a plastic storage shed. Beyond the patio were several acres filled with trees. Dozens of bird feeders adorned the branches, and birds of all kinds fluttered between the low-hanging branches. With some flowers and trimmed trees, it might look like paradise.

"My name is Mary," she called toward the backyard, though she didn't see anyone. "And this is my sister Betty."

A man walked slowly out from the other side of the storage shed. "It's a pleasure to make both of your acquaintances."

Mary tried not to stare, but she couldn't seem to help herself. "Yours as well," she finally said.

The man wore an army-green bathrobe, flannel pants, and dark brown moccasins. His face was dotted with age spots, and his gray hair was almost gone. This was the man in Karly's photograph. This was Jacob.

Instead of looking at them, the man's eyes were focused on the birds in the trees. "Do you hear them? They're talking about the weather."

She glanced back at Betty, and her sister stepped toward her. The man turned to

302

Mary, his blue eyes staring beyond her, and she realized in that moment that the man might hear her and the birds, but he couldn't see them. Jacob was blind. She swallowed, forcing her tone to sound much lighter than she felt.

"Do the birds usually talk about the weather?" Mary asked.

"Only when a storm's moving in." He stepped closer to them. "Are you friends of Karly's?"

Mary nodded and then realized again that he couldn't see her. "We met Karly in Ivy Bay." A cool breeze blew in from the water, and she zipped up her jacket as she stepped toward him. "She's a lovely young woman." Mary meant it, despite her certainty that Karly had stolen her mother's letters.

"Have a seat," he offered with a wave toward the edge of the patio. "Are you the owner of the bookstore?" he asked.

"I am."

His smile was infectious. "She was so excited about taking those pictures of your shop. She said you went to bat for her."

"I didn't have to bat very hard. Her pictures were beautiful, and the writer loved her work."

"She does take nice pictures, doesn't she?" He laughed. "Not that I can see them. But

I know she's talented. She's won several contests with her photographs."

"She truly has a gift," Betty said.

"I wish I could see her pictures, but I began losing my sight almost forty years ago." His laugh was low, and he pressed his hands against his pants. "It's slowly disappeared, and now I can hardly see anything."

Mary glanced back at her sister. Betty was looking at Jacob with pity in her eyes. There were so many questions racing through Mary's mind that she wasn't quite sure where to start.

"Karly has a natural eye for taking pictures of the coast," Mary said carefully. "Her style reminds me of the pictures you used to paint."

He coughed and then tipped his head slightly. "Did Karly tell you I used to paint?"

"No." She hesitated. "My sister and I, we've been looking for a man — an artist — by the name of Stuart Hendricks."

He dropped into a plastic chair. "I guess you know that you've found him. Why are you looking for me?"

Mary reached for another of the plastic patio chairs and moved it near him. Then she moved a seat over for Betty to sit on the other side. Betty brushed the dirt off with her hands and sat down.

"We're also looking for a man named Jacob. Jacob Stuart Drew."

"Jacob Drew . . ." His voice trailed off and he turned, like he was looking out at the birds again.

Betty glanced over at her, worry in her eyes, but Mary held up one of her fingers, signaling for her to wait. The two of them waited, the birds' singing blending with the wind.

Finally, he cleared his throat, and he pressed his lips together before he spoke again. "Who did you say you were?"

"I'm Betty Nelson Emerson," her sister said, reaching for his hand. He trembled as she shook it.

"And I'm Mary Nelson Fisher."

"Ah," he replied as he sat back in his chair. "Essy Randlett's girls."

Mary exchanged a glance with Betty, her heart beating a little faster.

She tried to be patient, waiting for him to say more, but he was so quiet that she wondered for a moment if he had stopped breathing. His chest continued to rise and fall under his robe, though, his lips trembling ever so slightly. Even though he couldn't see her or Betty, it was a bit unnerving to her that he could probably hear their slightest movement, even the slightest breath. She tried very hard to keep her breathing as steady as possible. She didn't want him to know how nervous she felt at this moment.

Part of her wanted to like this man in front of her, a man who listened to the birds sing, who appreciated Karly and her photography and was excited about her work. Another part of her had a hard time forgetting what he'd led their mother to do.

He scooted his chair closer to her. "Is your mother still alive?"

She shook her head even though he couldn't see. "She went to be with the Lord five years ago."

He turned his head toward them again, his voice sad as he seemed to process her words. "I'm really sorry to hear that."

"She lived a full life. A good life."

"She was a good woman." He brushed his hands over his robe. "How did you find me?"

"We found some letters that Mom wrote to you."

His lips curled with a giant smile. "You found the missing letters?"

Mary glanced over at Betty. "We didn't realize they'd been missing."

"There were eight of them," he said.

"The woman who bought your studio after you found eight books in the cellar, books you designed for Hartell Press, and she brought them to me by coincidence."

He sighed, and for a moment, Mary thought he might cry. "I've been looking for them for so long —"

"Did you leave them behind when you moved?" Mary asked.

"I must have. I was in my midforties when I began to lose my eyesight. I couldn't exactly paint anymore, so I sold the studio. They must have been left behind. When I couldn't find them, I asked my niece who'd helped me move, and she said she had thrown the box out. But now — I wonder if she was thinking of a different box? I don't know. But I'm glad to have them back."

A bird landed on the table, and Stuart turned his head toward it. A gentle call slipped out of his lips, and the bird turned toward him, tweeting something in return.

"This one's a talker," he said before he made the whistle sound one more time.

"Jacob," Mary said, reaching into her purse. "Can I ask you something else?"

"I have a feeling you're going to, no matter what I say," he said, a faint smile on his face. "Essy was like that too."

Mary pulled the bracelet out of her purse

and placed it gently in his hand.

"Oh dear," was all he said in response to the slight jangle of the jewels.

"Is this one of the pieces of jewelry you and our mom stole from the Willards?"

Jacob's head sagged, and his chin rested on his chest. "She still had it, after all these years?"

"What happened to the rest of it, Jacob?"

"It's Stuart now."

A boat sounded on the water, the sound of its horn rippling up to the porch.

"I sold everything. That was why we did it in the first place, to pay for my sister's care. She almost died several times, and my father couldn't afford the new treatments on his income. I tried to make enough money for her treatments by drawing pictures of people around town. I saved every penny that I made, but it wasn't nearly enough to help her."

A sparrow landed at the end of the porch, watching them. "I can't imagine how difficult that must have been," Mary said.

"When you're eighteen, you think you're invincible — at least that's what I thought. The Willard family commissioned me to draw a series of pictures of their family, and one night while I was there, their daughter took some jewelry from the safe to wear while I drew her picture."

Mary could almost see him in the Willards' home, watching Ruthanne unlock the safe and then remembering the combination. He must have been torn between what was right and what seemed right. What if Betty had contracted something like tuberculosis when they were children? What if she was going to die? Would Mary have been tempted to do the same? It was easy to judge someone when you weren't standing in his or her shoes. She didn't know what she would do if she felt responsible for keeping Betty alive.

"The night of the party," he continued, "the Willards asked me to draw portraits of their friends, so I walked around on both floors of their home, drawing different scenes and pictures. When I was alone in the upstairs den, I filled my bag of art supplies with cash and jewelry as well. And then I went outside, hopped in the car, and drove away."

"Mom drove the car," Mary said, and Stuart nodded.

"Our mother, the getaway driver," Betty mused. "Who would have ever thought?"

Mary tried to imagine her mother, young and in love, risking her whole future for a thief. A desperate man driven to steal to

309

save his sister's life. But a thief, no less.

"A couple of weeks later, I gave the money to my parents."

"Surely, they suspected," Mary said.

"I'm sure they did, but we were all desperate to help Patty."

A cool breeze blew across the porch. Mary fastened another button on her jacket.

"Of course it was wrong. I know that now," he said. "It was dumb. I was just a kid. But I thought maybe they wouldn't notice somehow."

"Why did our mother have the bracelet?" Mary asked. "Why didn't you sell that along with the rest of the jewelry?"

Stuart turned the bracelet over in his hand, running his fingers over the faces of the gems.

"I slipped it into her purse. I wanted her to have something, just in case. Something she could have if she ever needed money." He laid the bracelet down gently on the table. "Looking back, I see how silly that was. Essy would never have pawned stolen jewelry. She wasn't a criminal, not like me. I'm not sure when she found it. I wasn't sure she ever had."

"You never asked her?" Mary said.

He shook his head. "After that night . . ." He cleared his throat and seemed to struggle to find words to convey his meaning. "After that night, things changed between us. I think Essy hadn't really thought it through when she agreed to drive. She just thought it was a lark, a harmless prank. She was like that, you now? Carefree. Kind of immature. But once we'd done it, once the jewelry was sold, she realized what we'd done. When she saw what happened to the Willards after that, it just tore her up."

Mary recalled what Teresa had said about the robbery making the Willards lose everything. Knowing you'd caused that would be a heavy burden to bear.

"She couldn't look at me. She still loved me, I know she did. She wanted us to be together. But I was a reminder of what she'd done, and she felt trapped. If she turned herself in, she would get me in trouble too, and my family depended on me. She knew Patty wasn't going to make it if I wasn't there to help them. So she struggled with her guilt in silence."

Mary tried to imagine what her mother must have gone through, holding in a secret of that magnitude. Was she ever tempted to confess? Did she ever imagine going to Ruthanne and telling her exactly what happened and returning the bracelet? Mary knew her mother had developed a deep faith

311

by the time she was born. Surely, she would have confessed her crime to God. But did she ever really feel forgiven?

"We broke up soon after that. My parents went away, taking Patty to a sanatorium in Colorado. It saved her. She lived for four more decades after that. When they left, I joined the army. The war was over, but they were glad to have me. I went away, and when I came back, I went by my middle name. My mother had remarried after I was born, to Patty's father, so my last name had changed from Drew to Hendricks ages before. I felt like a different person, so I decided to be one. I started drawing again. A few publishers liked what I sent them, and I began to design book covers at first, and then began selling my paintings in galleries."

Mary looked back out at the birds. "Why didn't you go to Colorado after you got out of the army?"

Stuart shrugged. "This was home. I didn't go out much, but I got married, had a couple of kids, but my wife and I . . . things weren't what they should have been between us. That was probably my fault. I shouldn't have married one woman when I was still in love with another."

Mary's bad feelings for this man had dissipated, replaced by compassion for the agony that he had endured in his heart, mind, and body. He'd started out with such a promising life — football star, artist, and a man devoted to his family — and then life had thrown him a terrible curveball. Or perhaps he had thrown the ball himself. She didn't know if God would have given Patty and her family another way to get her treatment for her tuberculosis or if his sister would have slipped from this world, leaving a young Jacob racked with guilt over what he hadn't done to help her.

This man had brought light to many with his artwork, and it seemed that he'd been kind to Karly as well. With God's forgiveness, and the freedom of the truth, perhaps he could live his remaining years free of his guilt.

"Did you ever want to confess?" Mary asked quietly.

"Every day of my life." Stuart sighed.

Betty leaned forward. "Thankfully, God can forgive our sins even when we struggle to forgive ourselves."

Mary fingered the bracelet that lay between them. "And there is someone for whom it would mean a great deal to know what happened that night."

"Ruthanne. We went to school together."

313

He tilted his head, as if listening to some far-off sound. "But what good would it do after all this time?"

"I think, to Ruthanne Willard Porter, it would mean a great deal to hear you say you're sorry."

"And you could return the bracelet," Betty added.

And Mary was sure the statute of limitations had long passed on this crime. If Stuart returned the bracelet now, she was pretty sure he wasn't going to be arrested for it.

"You think so?"

"I do."

They sat in silence for a few minutes, enjoying the birdsong.

"Mom didn't forget you," Betty said quietly.

Mary looked at Betty. She wasn't sure what her sister was going to say, but she suspected it would mean a lot to Jacob to hear it.

"She loved our father very much, but she collected the Hartell books with your artwork."

He bunched up a tissue in his fist. "How do you think she knew they were mine?"

"Maybe she recognized your style," Betty suggested. "It is fairly distinctive. She treasured those books."

"I kept every one of her letters," Stuart said. "Except the ones that got lost, of course. But I have the rest. I kept one in each book I ever worked on for Hartell."

"It's a strange filing system you have," Betty said.

Stuart shrugged. "I always knew where to find them, and I figured I was less likely to lose a whole library of books than a stack of paper."

"A whole library of books? How many letters are there?"

"Eighty-six in all," he said with a smile.

"You did the covers for that many books?" Mary asked, her mouth hanging open.

"I did the art for a few dozen," Stuart said. "The rest, I just did the typesetting on." He smiled. "You said you tracked me down because you found your mother's letters. Did you bring those here?"

"I'm afraid not," Mary said. "Someone took them from my store."

"Took them?" he said. "Who would do something like that?"

The screen door slammed behind her, and Mary jumped. Turning, she saw Karly walk toward them, her long hair windblown around her shoulders. She glanced at all three of them, and then looked at her grandfather. "I took the letters."

"You took them?" Stuart repeated her words like he couldn't believe them. "I don't understand."

Karly lifted one of the chairs from the sunporch and carried it outside. Sitting down beside him, she reached for his hand. "Grandpa Stuart's been wondering about those books for years, and I wanted to get the missing letters for him. He never really got over —"

Her voice broke, and Mary reached out to take her hand. She admired her love for her grandfather, but stealing, even with the intent to help another, would only hurt her in the long run. It was a lesson they'd all learned today.

"Thank you for trying to help me out," Stuart told Karly. "But you shouldn't have stolen those letters. They weren't yours to take."

He went silent for a moment, and all Mary could hear was the chirp of the birds in the trees around them. Then, slowly, he pushed himself up to standing. Karly lunged forward to help him, but he waved her away.

"Grandpa, what are you doing?" Karly followed him as he started to shuffle toward the house. Mary looked at Betty, who appeared as confused as she felt.

"I'm listening to my own advice," he said

as he reached the door. "I'm tired of living like this. They're not going to put an old man in prison, and even if they do, that's okay. It's finally time. I'm going to confess."

TWENTY-TWO

Jacob — Stuart, Mary had to start calling him Stuart — changed into a striped button-down shirt and dress slacks to "look respectable."

"The letters are in my trunk," Karly said as they waited for him to get dressed. "I didn't want to take them from you, especially after all you did for me, but I felt like I had no other choice. When I realized you'd found Grandpa's missing books, I was terrified, and then I panicked when I saw the letters."

Mary straightened her seat belt over her hips. The irony was that if Karly hadn't taken the letters, it would have taken Mary much longer to find Stuart Hendricks. Instead of hiding the truth, Karly had led her straight to it.

"You don't have to worry." Karly put her sunglasses on. "I'll tell Jayne what happened tomorrow."

Mary turned toward her. "Why would you tell Jayne?"

"I want her to know the truth before I resign."

"Oh no," Mary said, shaking her head. "Jayne will lose her mind if you resign from your position. Then she'll be angry at me for taking you away. You need to stay until they leave for Europe, at least."

"You're not going to tell them what I did?"

"I don't know why they would have to know."

There were two cars in the driveway of the gray Victorian house attached to Willards'. Mary got out of the car before the others so they wouldn't overwhelm the family, and she knocked on the front door. Ruthanne's daughter-in-law Teresa answered her knock, greeting her with a bit of hesitation. "I don't work on weekends."

"Oh no," Mary said. "I don't need anything repaired. You said I should come back and visit your mother-in-law again."

"Of course," Teresa said. "Well, in that case, come in."

Mary gestured for the others to join her, and they went inside. Teresa introduced Mary to her husband, Bradley, a handsome man with thick black hair. He greeted her with a friendly handshake and introduced her to a thinner version of himself, his son Cody, who he said was a film major in college. Cody's handshake was just as friendly as his father's.

Ruthanne was sitting in a rocking chair in front of the card table. She rocked, put together a piece of the puzzle, and rocked again. Her gaze traveled past Mary, not seeming to recognize her from earlier this week, but she stopped rocking when she saw Stuart walk into the living room. She stared at him like he was a ghost. "I know you."

"Hello, Ruthanne," he replied. "It's good to see you again."

The weight of his words seemed to settle on all of them except Ruthanne. The artist who'd painted the Willard family picture couldn't see any of them.

"Jacob," she whispered, seeming to recognize his voice. "Jacob Drew."

She searched the room until she found her son. "This is Jacob. The man who painted the picture over our mantel."

Bradley stepped forward to shake Stuart's outstretched hand. "It's a pleasure to meet you, sir."

"Are you here to visit with our mother?" Teresa asked.

"Actually, I have something to return to her." He reached into his pocket. "To return to all of you."

From his pocket, he pulled out the diamond and emerald bracelet that Mary had found, and Teresa gasped.

Mary helped him walk over to Ruthanne and place the bracelet on the card table in front of her. "This belongs to you, Ruthanne."

Her fingers stretched out, taking the jewels, gingerly touching each diamond and emerald. Then she held it up to her necklace. Mary's heart was filled with joy at the sight of Ruthanne being reunited with her family's heirloom. When Ruthanne looked up at them again, there were tears in her eyes. "You found it."

When Bradley spoke again, the friendliness was gone. "Where did you find this?"

"I didn't find it," Stuart explained with a shake of his head. Mary felt for him and his agony at having to explain what he'd done. "A long time ago, I took it."

Teresa collapsed onto the sofa, but Bradley stepped closer to him. "What do you mean?"

"Seventy years ago, I stole it from your family's safe, along with the cash and other jewelry that was inside." Stuart's head was still turned toward Ruthanne as the elderly woman watched him. "I am so sorry."

"You were the one who robbed my family." Bradley's voice escalated. "You were the one who destroyed our family's inheritance."

Mary glanced at Teresa, hoping the woman might help her husband calm his voice, but she looked just as angry as he did. Her arms were crossed, and she was glaring at the man.

When his voice broke, Karly stepped forward. "My grandfather is asking for your forgiveness and would like to do whatever he can to repay you."

"My mother slaved for years at this sewing shop to help provide for our family. All her plans were destroyed. How could he ever repay that?"

Ruthanne blinked, looking to her son. "I didn't slave, Bradley. I loved my work at the shop."

Mary realized the man was also thinking about the difference that money would have made in his own life, and she couldn't blame him.

"Where did you spend the money?" Bradley asked.

"At a sanatorium in Colorado Springs."

Stuart's words silenced all of them. He continued to tell them about his sister, and about how the money he'd taken had saved her life.

"I've got to call my attorney," Bradley said before he stomped out of the room.

"You can call the police instead," Stuart offered.

Teresa shook her head. "We're not going to call the police."

Teresa followed her husband out of the room, leaving Cody and his grandmother with them. Cody studied Karly for a moment, and then he looked at Stuart. "It will take them some time to process this information. But our family lost a bunch of money during the eighties, and even if they'd still had this stuff, I'm guessing this money would have been lost too."

"How is Patty?" Ruthanne said, looking up at Stuart again with clear eyes.

"She passed on over twenty years ago."

"I'm sorry to hear of it. She was the sweetest little girl." She slipped the bracelet onto her arm and then looked at Stuart again. "Thank you, Jacob. I knew one day you'd bring this back to me."

They were all shocked into silence. Ruthanne had known all along that it had been Jacob? Had she kept it quiet all this time?

Ruthanne gave Stuart a smile, and even though Mary didn't totally understand, she knew all was forgiven.

A young couple pushed a baby stroller into Mary's Mystery Bookshop at the beginning of January, gawking at the shelves of books and the children's reading area. In his right hand, the man clutched a copy of the latest edition of *Cape Cod Living.*

"It's just as cute as the writer said," the woman whispered, but Mary heard her words and smiled. She was glad that this couple and dozens of other tourists before them were enjoying the store. Harrison had done an excellent job describing the bookshop as small and eclectic, with the mysteries for adults and a myriad of books for children. Karly's pictures captured the setting just perfectly. When the story came out a week before, she'd asked Betty to replenish the flowers, and her sister had done another beautiful job bringing spring into the store even as it snowed outside. The phone hadn't stopped ringing with requests for hours and directions, and she'd made enough money to keep Gus in his preferred salmon for months to come.

The young woman held out the magazine, pointing at Mary's picture. "Is this you?"

"It is," Mary replied with a grin, though she thought she looked much older in the photo than she was. Next time, she'd ask Karly to bring makeup with her too.

"We read the article on your shop, and we just had to come to Ivy Bay."

"Stay as long as you'd like," Mary said. "There's a great diner across the street if you decide you want lunch. And several wonderful bed-and-breakfasts."

The door opened, and Henry rushed into the store. "My daughter Kimberly just called," he said. "She told me we're supposed to get a foot of snow tonight. I thought I'd hop on over to Stuart's place and make sure he's got everything he needs in case the power goes out." He leaned toward the counter. "When I get back, I'm taking you to lunch."

"Oh, I'm much too busy today to go to lunch."

Rebecca came around the corner. "Please take her to lunch, Henry. She hasn't had a break in days."

"See you in two hours." He waved over his shoulder as the door chimes spilled out into the street. He wasn't going to let her decline his lunch invitation, and she supposed she was glad of it.

She turned back toward Rebecca who answered the questions in her eyes with an innocent shrug. "It's true," Rebecca said.

"You need a break and you need to spend some time with Henry."

It was kind of Henry to check on Stuart, but she didn't know if Stuart would be at the house today. Karly had been taking him over for frequent visits with Ruthanne, who seemed to be quite lucid during their times together, though she hadn't figured out yet that Stuart was blind.

The door opened again, and this time Betty walked through. In her arms, she carried a box, not much different in size than the cardboard box full of books that had led her to Stuart.

"What do you have?" Mary asked, trying to peek into the box.

"Follow me," Betty said with a wave.

Betty put the box up on the counter, and she took out a beautiful book that was covered with a green marble color. On it was embossed in a cursive font *Lost Letters of Love.*

Mary opened the cover and printed inside were the copies of her mother's letters to Stuart that she'd scanned.

"I made one for us," Betty explained. "And one for Stuart."

Mary brushed her hand over the marbled pages. "It's perfect."

"I felt a little guilty making these, like I

was betraying Dad, but then I realized the woman in these letters was the woman he fell in love with as well." The letters were not only a gift to Stuart. Mary turned the pages gently, admiring her mother's neat handwriting and the sweet sentiments she'd recorded.

"Mom would have been pleased to see this, Betty."

Mary flipped to the letter that Essy had written after the robbery, the one that had made her suspect Jacob was Betty's father. It was still strange to imagine her mother like that, scared and guilty, but still so clearly in love.

"You definitely gave me a scare with that one." Betty laughed, gesturing to the open page. Mary ran her hand across the smooth surface of the paper. "For a while, I actually believed . . ." She let her voice trail off.

"You were right, though," Mary said. "About judging a book by its cover. I had made up my mind about what the letter meant, and I couldn't see past it." She stroked the soft paper. "I misjudged them both."

"It was easy to see why you did," Betty said softly.

Mary nodded. "You know, it wouldn't have changed anything if it had been true."

"It would have changed a lot of things," Betty said, then gently closed the book and looked up at Mary. "But it wouldn't have changed the most important thing."

"We'll always be sisters," Mary said, smiling at Betty.

"Nothing is ever going to change that."

Mary hugged her sister again. She was more grateful for her sister than she knew. No one else understood her and knew her like Betty, and her heart swelled with love.

"Not everyone is lucky enough to have their best friend be their sister," Betty said softly. "We are so blessed."

Looking around her shop at Rebecca and at the lifelong dream that had finally come true the day she'd opened the bookshop, Mary couldn't agree more.

"We are blessed indeed."

A CONVERSATION WITH
ELIZABETH ADAMS

Q: *What draws you to Mary's Mystery Book-shop as a writer?*

A: I've spent a lot of time in Cape Cod, and I love the slower pace of life, the beauty of the landscape and the towns, and the sense of history that pervades everything. I love watching the sun rise over cranberry bogs and set over a rocky beach. Working on this book was like a vacation to my favorite place. But I didn't have to pack and do laundry beforehand!

Q: *Which character in the series do you most relate to?*

A: I have a young daughter, so I think I probably relate to Rebecca as she struggles to balance her job and her family — and tries to squeeze in some writing in her spare time! Also, like Ashley, my daughter is exceptionally smart and funny and help-ful and a joy to be around. It's possible that's just a mama's pride talking, but I really did love working on the scenes with Rebecca and Ashley in them.

Q: *If you could open a bookshop anywhere, where would it be? And what kind of bookshop would it be?*

A: I fear that bookstores are mostly a losing business proposition these days. With so many other entertainment options — TV, movies, video games, the Internet — fewer people are buying books. It would take a brave soul to open an independent bookstore in this day and age. That's why it's important to support your favorite authors and publishers by buying books new so they can continue to afford to produce them!

Q: *What is your favorite mystery book/author? Why?*

A: My current favorite author is Tana French. She writes these totally engrossing, atmospheric mysteries set in Ireland. Once you start reading one of her books, you can't stop!

Q: *Have you ever had to solve a mystery? Tell us about it!*

A: Most of the mysteries in my life are along

the lines of "Who drank the last of the milk?" and "Why are there no clean towels?" But I hope that I do get to solve a mystery someday. I like to think I would be good at it.

Q: *Mary loves to make new ice-cream flavors and enjoys reading mystery novels. What are some of your hobbies?*

A: I like to eat ice cream and read mystery novels.

Q: *Please tell us about your family!*

A: I have two cats. They're hilariously smart and devious and they inspired me when I was writing about Gus. I'd just think, *What would my cats do in this situation?* The answer was usually *Turn up their noses and ignore me,* so that's what Gus does a lot of in this book.

SWEET SUSAN'S
VANILLA CUPCAKES

1 1/2 cups self-rising flour
1 1/4 cups all-purpose flour
Pinch of salt
1 cup unsalted butter, at room temperature
2 cups sugar
4 large eggs, at room temperature
1 cup milk
1 tablespoon vanilla extract

Preheat oven to 350 degrees. Line two muffin tins with cupcake papers.

In a small bowl, combine the flours and salt. Set aside.

In the large bowl of an electric mixer, cream the butter until smooth. Add the sugar a little at a time and beat until fluffy, or for about three minutes. Add the eggs, one at a time, beating well after each addition. Add the milk and vanilla, and beat until smooth. Add the flour mixture in two batches, beating just until the ingredients are incorporated. Scrape down the batter with a rubber spatula to make sure the ingredients are well blended. Carefully spoon the batter into the cupcake liners, filling them about three-quarters full. Bake for twenty to twenty-five minutes, or until a cake tester inserted into the center of a cupcake comes out clean.

Cool the cupcakes for fifteen minutes, then remove from the tins and cool completely. Frost with icing, recipe below.

Icing:

1 cup (2 sticks) unsalted butter
6–8 cups confectioners' sugar
1/2 cup milk
2 teaspoons vanilla extract
Food coloring in your favorite color

Place the butter in the bowl of an electric mixer. Add four cups of the sugar, and then pour in the milk and the vanilla. Beat on medium speed for three to five minutes, or until smooth and creamy. Gradually add the remaining sugar, one-half cup at a time, beating well after each addition, until the icing is thick enough to spread. You may not need to add all the sugar. If desired, add a few drops of food coloring and mix thoroughly. Icing can be stored in an airtight container for up to three days.

ABOUT THE AUTHOR

Elizabeth Adams lives in New York City with her husband. When she's not writing, she spends her time playing with their rambunctious daughter, cleaning up after two devious cats, and trying to find time to read mysteries.